World's Deadliest School Trips

The Great White Bear

James DuBern

Published in 2021 by Amazon KDP Publishing.

©2021 James DuBern.

james@poptacular.com

Cover illustration © Kateryna Kirdoglo. All rights reserved.

Formatting and copy editing by Naomi Munts Proofreading.

Contents

Chapter 1

March 1975

In an icy parking lot outside the high school in Matagami, a small yellow school bus was awaiting its passengers. It was late March, and while the rest of the northern hemisphere was enjoying the first daffodils of spring, here in Quebec it snowed on a daily basis. Even at mid-afternoon on day like this, the sun couldn't melt the icicles that hung from every roof. This place was literally freezing, and that's before the bus headed north.

Lance, a slight boy of twelve years old, retrieved his backpack and paintbox from his parents' car and carefully set them down on the cold, cracked pavement. He hugged his mum tightly, resting his head on her shoulder. From the driver's seat of their beige wood-panelled car, his dad watched them in the side mirror and shook his head. When Lance's father was twelve, he had been out hunting and playing war with his friends, not painting and hugging his mother. So he kept telling his son, anyhow.

"I don't want to go, Mom," Lance whispered in her ear. "Can't I just stay home with you? And why isn't Mrs Cooke coming?"

"She's sick. But the principal said it's fine without her. Bob is going to drop you off - maybe he'll stay. And there are two staff up there, who I'm sure are quite capable of looking after six children."

"It's for the best," she added, holding his shoulders at arm's length. "You must make new friends. This is our home now. If you get anxious, you have your paints. Oh, and here's your lunch." She passed him a brown paper bag, folded over neatly at the top.

"A week will fly by and you will have a great time, I'm sure of it. Well, it's better than being stuck home with your brothers, right?"

He nodded and scooped up his heavy backpack, causing him to stagger unsteadily. A snigger of laughter came from a group of lads waiting nearby.

Lance's father surveyed the scene outside the school and watched his son's classmates as they jostled together. Two of the boys fenced with icicles, while the third kid lobbed a snowball at a couple of girls. 'Why did my son grow up to be such a weakling?' he wondered, irritably. In the rear-view mirror he watched his wife say goodbye to Lance. He beeped the horn and beckoned her over, attracting the attention of everyone in the car park. His wife hurried into the passenger seat. Lance's father didn't say goodbye to his son; and instead used the moment to lecture his wife on the effects of mollycoddling.

All that remained outside Delta High School was a small yellow school bus, six kids and Bob, the driver.

Lance reached down to pick up his wooden paintbox. With the heavy backpack counterbalancing him like a crane, he knew if he reached down too low he'd topple over in front of the hockey boys. The worst possible start to the trip.

The briefcase-sized paint box was his pride and joy – a gift from his mum for Christmas and his birthday combined. Sixteen tubes of acrylic paint arranged in a gorgeous rainbow from crimson red through cerulean blue to burnt sienna. Anticipating that he might paint a polar bear in snow, Lance had brought extra tubes of titanium white. The set also had a cardboard colour wheel, a curved wooden mixing palette and a trio of hog's hair paintbrushes.

His favourite pastime was to paint landscapes around his hometown of Matagami. It was so far north in the Canadian wilderness that there seemed to be just two seasons – a brief, mosquito-infested flash of summer, and a fierce sub-Arctic winter that dragged on like a cough you couldn't kick. In the six months he had lived there, Lance had begun to appreciate the nuances of an overcast sky. He could pick out the lavender tones in pregnant snow clouds, or the warm wisps of amber as the low winter sun fought its way through. He loved to paint big skies and distant jagged peaks. If only Matagami had interesting foregrounds that he could walk to. There were only so many times he could paint the local Center Civique, with its rare splash of red on the sign for the bowling alley. This week held the promise of painting an animal in the wild – a polar bear, no less.

He slid his paintbox into the back of the bus, being careful to keep it flat, and put his backpack on top. He kicked through the salty slush and climbed the black rubberised steps. From his seat near the front, he watched his parents pull onto the highway and return home. He opened the brown paper bag to reveal an apple, and a peanut butter and jelly sandwich wrapped neatly in aluminium foil. Tucked among them was a Rubik's Cube. He inspected it with joyful excitement. It had light scratches and the black plastic was worn slightly matt. He guessed his mum had got it from a swap meet. It was new to him though, and as he squeezed it tight, he felt his mum's kindness through the colourful plastic faces. He felt sick at the idea of being separated from her for a whole week.

"Load up, y'all. We're heading out in five," shouted Bob. He was the caretaker of the school who had been persuaded to give up his Saturday to drive the kids to James Bay, five hours north of Matagami.

The two girls – both in the year above Lance – slung their cases into the back and climbed into the vehicle. They nodded politely to Lance and took seats on different sides.

The remaining trio of boys threw their backpacks on top of the stack behind the back seats. Lance had seen these boys playing hockey for the school. In the rest of the world it would be described more fully as ice hockey, but in Quebec the ice was a given.

Freddy precariously balanced his bag on top of the luggage mountain when a shout of "Don't block the windows, son!" came from up front. He rolled his eyes and yanked his backpack out, causing the stack of bags to avalanche onto the wet tarmac. Along with them came the curious wooden box, dragged out in a tangle of buckles. It cracked open like a book as it hit the ground, scattering the tubes of paint onto the ice.

Freddy huffed and shoved the backpacks back in, slamming the yellow door to stop them cascading out once more.

He climbed on board and snatched Lance's Rubik's Cube on the way past, yanking it so high that it dinged the metal ceiling of the bus.

"What's this?" he muttered, taking it to the back seat, where he joined his friends.

Lance reddened with frustration at being robbed but was unable to get any words out. By the time he sheepishly put his hand up to get Bob's attention, Freddy was at the back of the bus fighting over the plastic toy with his friend Knievel.

The bus door slammed shut and Bob – who the kids only knew vaguely – took his seat. He looked in the bulging rear view mirror and counted six passengers. He shouted in a gruff but friendly voice, gaining all their attention.

"So you're the lucky ones who got chosen, eh? Five- or six-hour drive, and that's if this weather holds up. Bathroom break is in three hours at Wichika Springs. Until there, I don't wanna hear any fighting or shouting. You got that?"

The kids nodded.

Bob stirred the engine into life and the old yellow bus shook. As it pulled away, Freddy punched Knievel in the shoulder, to draw his attention to the back window. The box of paints was still on the ground, gathering a shower of slush from the wheels. "Ooops," he said, to which Knievel sniggered.

Jack, a big-built kid who took the third row of the bus, shook his head. "Bozos," he said dismissively.

"So, you kids are off to see a polar bear, I hear," shouted Bob as he clunked through the noisy gears. He looked back at the sea of faces in his mirror.

"Remember. If it's black, fight back. If it's brown, lie down. If it's white..."

"Goodnight," the kids groaned, having heard this classic bear advice a hundred times.

Bob laughed and hunkered down to the relentless job of driving from morning until night. He hoped to get there and back in a long day, because his beloved hockey team – the Montreal Canadiens – were playing against the Chicago Black Hawks that evening. He didn't mind though. Since his wife passed away, he preferred to keep busy.

Lance, ever the keen artist, mapped out the bus on a scrap of paper; five rows of benches with an aisle carved down the middle. Lance sat on the second row where he could see past Bob to the road ahead. Directly behind him sat Victoria, with Dyani to her left. Jack sat by himself on the fourth row, and Knievel and Freddy took up the back row, where they fought constantly.

As the bus left the town of Matagami, Dyani hopped from her seat to the bench where Lance sat. He did a double take, then squeezed up towards the window, resuming his focus on a tiny spider. He rotated his palm this way and that, and gently let it walk from one hand to the other.

Dyani was also an outsider at the school. She was of First Nation descent, unlike her schoolmates whose families had come from the big cities to work the mines. She found it ironic to feel a lack of belonging, given that it was her ancestors – the James Bay Cree – that had lived in this region for thousands of years.

Despite Freddy's constant teasing, her family did not live in a tipi – those days were a hundred years past. Their simple log home had been built by Dyani's grandparents when Matagami was just a handful of cabins on the lake. With three generations living under one roof, the family continued their traditions of hunting, guiding and trapping in the wilderness. Dyani was the first of her family to attend an English high school. It felt like she had one foot in the future and one in the past. Sometimes the stretch was uncomfortable.

"Are you okay?" she asked, her voice barely audible over the rumble of the engine and the sports radio.

Lance nodded, focusing on the spider. Dyani continued, "Take no notice of Freddie and Knievel".

He looked at Dyani, whom he recognised from school, although she was in the year above. She wore a thick, hand-knitted cardigan with a diagonal pattern and an eagle on the front. Her hair was long and black, and her eyes were as dark as he'd ever seen.

"Knievel?" he asked.

"Well, his name's Kevin, but everyone calls him Knievel after the stuntman. You know what they say; if you're gonna be dumb, you better be tough."

Lance smiled.

"Guys like that; they have to assert their dominance. Like bears," Dyani said.

"Blame evolution?" Lance asked, making his hand into a claw.

Her eyes opened wide. "Yes. They like everyone to know this is their territory and they can take what they like. But you know what? It's our territory too. We have to stand up for ourselves."

Lance transferred to the spider to the window, and gazed out at a vast snowfield that covered a lake. "You sound like my dad. His solution to everything is to fight back. Like it's my fault for not retaliating. But – look at them. They all play hockey and wrestle. It really would be like me fighting a bear."

The bus was buzzing with chatter and the engine rumbled loudly. Dyani and Lance continued to talk quietly, with pensive gaps between their sentences.

There was no sense in rushing anything with a five-hour drive ahead.

"So your dad says fight. What about your mom; what does she suggest?"

"My dad barks at her constantly too, so we just keep out of their way. She says when someone's mad, something is making them mad. If you can understand that, you can forgive them. Even help them. Get inside their heads, you know?"

Dyani nodded. "So your mom thinks it's in their head, and your dad thinks it's in their blood."

"Yes. That sounds about right. I'm Lance, by the way. I'm new. Well, we've been at Matagami for six months now, so kinda new."

"I know who you are!" She laughed. "There are like a hundred kids in our school; you can't hide here! By the way, I saw your painting they put up in the reception at the school. You're really good."

Lance smiled shyly. He painted when he was worried. It helped clear his head. Since he'd moved to Matagami six months ago, he had been painting a lot.

"Can you believe we're going to see a polar bear?" Dyani asked, sketching one on Lance's piece of paper with a biro. Its legs were oddly square and its neck too short, but Lance smiled at it approvingly and asked her if she wanted to play a game. They spent the next

16

couple of hours playing hangman on scraps of paper until there were no white areas left to scrawl on.

Victoria, in the row behind, was watching intently. She thought Dyani's polar bear looked like an alien pig and would have told her so. For nearly two hours she was the third hangman player, just without them knowing. She was winning too, according to a tally in her mind. When the game was over, Victoria sat in silence watching the endless forests fly past. She would focus ahead on a bridge or sign and watch it come in slowly, then faster and faster until it whizzed past at 60 miles per hour.

Knievel, Freddy and Jack sang more loudly as the journey went on, until Bob had to shout to make the noise stop. The volume crept up, up, up, then down. Over and over again.

Chapter 2

The Middle of Nowhere

The bus pushed tirelessly along the James Bay Road towards its northern terminus; the body of water after which it was named. James Bay is an offshoot of a gigantic inland sea called Hudson Bay.

The combination of being far north and relatively shallow means it freezes from November to June. The polar bears spend their winter on the ice floes, hunting for seals when they surface for air. In the summer when the ice melts, they are forced to the shores, where they sleep in the shade of the rocky coastlines, conserving their precious energy. Our story takes place in James Bay in the spring of 1975, and although the ice had another couple of months before it fully broke up, a bear was splitting its time between the ice sheets and the shoreline around Fort Lagrave.

The James Bay Road had barely anything to distinguish one mile from the next. On both sides were forests as far as the eye could see. The desolate gravel road, dusted with snow and only the occasional dirty tracks from a supply truck, reminded Lance of the journey his family had taken just six months ago. They had rented out their house in the suburbs of Ottawa so Dad could take a job with the mining company in Matagami. They'd loaded their car until the suspension creaked and set off into Canada's great interior, arriving eventually at the one-horse town of Matagami.

The main highway that ran through town had the high school, which some kids drove an hour to get to, a community centre, a movie theatre and a bowling alley. Aside from that were a few stores, a gas station and the promise of a new life full of outdoor adventure. The town was a mixture of ramshackle cabins, which were still inhabited by solitary old-timers, and new estates of identical homes that had sprung up in the last ten years as the zinc mine drew in workers. At least, thought Lance, their home was one of the new ones.

"You get your own bedrooms, and a bathroom *just* for you boys. Quit your whining!" his dad had said. He liked to constantly remind his sons how lucky they were. But Lance wasn't desperate for a bathroom; he wanted the friends he'd had to say goodbye to in Ottawa.

Back on the bus, Lance and Dyani were all talked out. Even the brawlers at the back were now sleeping, dribbling into the collars of their hockey shirts. Bob the driver listened to sports and sipped at a huge thermos flask of coffee that seemed to last forever.

It takes a particularly long and boring journey to make you excited about a petrol station, and this was one such trip. Canada's boreal forest is the largest on earth – even bigger than the Amazon rainforest – and by the time they reached that precious truck stop, the kids felt like they'd seen every last tree of it.

The doors slid open and the cold air snapped the children out of their torpor. The group staggered to their feet and had to relearn to walk as they descended the step onto the snowy pavement.

Lance walked up and down the aisles of the store, but he had not brought any money with him to buy anything. Freddy, it seemed, was in the same situation, and he slipped a chocolate bar into his pocket. He caught Lance's glance and stared viciously as if to kill any thoughts Lance might have of telling an adult.

Victoria, the quiet girl who had snooped on their hangman game, was transfixed by a hot dog grill. Under a hot amber light, metal rods rotated slowly, rolling the sausages over and over in their hot sun. She looked at the tiny cogs and chains that connected the rods to the motor and wondered how it worked. She had been given a screwdriver set by her grandfather several years ago and routinely took things apart. She just had to know how things worked or it would drive her nuts. She hated magicians. Bob disturbed her daydream and opened up the hot glass door, removing a leathery overcooked hot dog and placing it in a bun.

"You want one?" he asked Victoria, who shook her head and disappeared out of the store and back into her seat on the bus.

An icy, grubby snowball smacked Lance in the back of the neck as he returned to the vehicle. It managed to get right into the sliver of skin between his hat and his collar, and drips were now running down his spine. He turned and smiled as if he were in on the joke, and Freddy cackled triumphantly, tossing his chocolate bar wrapper into the wind.

They reboarded the bus, kicking their boots on the bottom step to leave the snow outside. The remainder of the journey passed uneventfully as the yellow bus gobbled up mile after mile of ruler-straight highway. Lance was grateful to have Dyani to talk to, and he enjoyed the peaceful hours when the thugs at the back of the bus slept.

Jack noticed Freddy and Knievel were passed out, and he reached over to pick the Rubik's Cube from next to them. Lance watched, and Jack smoothly tossed it across the aisle to him. Lance fumbled the catch and scooped it up off the floor, thanking Jack as he re-emerged. Three of the stickers were peeled off where Freddy had got frustrated with it and attempted to solve it by force. Presumably the glue had not held a second time, as now those stickers were missing and there were three black squares, rendering it useless.

"Don't worry, we can find the missing stickers. Or just paint them with your paints," Dyani suggested, seeing her travel companion's disappointment.

As they crept north in the rumbling yellow school bus, the terrain became more barren. The trees thinned out to make way for fields of rock and snow. Being near to the bay now, there were few hills or mountains, but they did see huge lakes, which were still iced over. What started as a light snow on the windscreen built steadily until the wipers looked beaten by the onslaught of thick, wet splats.

Lance focused far into the distance and watched the white specks flying towards the vehicle, imagining he was in one of his comic books, hurtling through outer space past stars and planets. Meanwhile, Victoria more soberly noted that their speed was down to 50 miles per hour and constantly recalculated the time it would take until they reached their destination. The kids cheered when the bus slowed to turn off the highway onto an unnamed road marked by a simple hand-painted sign saying:

Fort Lagrave
Access to James Bay (Summer Only)

The snowy road was narrow and treacherous, and the children now sat in unnerving silence as Bob had turned off the radio to concentrate. The bus puffed its way up the gentle slopes away from the highway, with rock-strewn snowfields on both sides.

At one point, so far from the James Bay Road that they could no longer see lights from occasional other vehicles, the bus stopped. Ahead lay an impassable snowdrift as big as the van itself.

"I've got three shovels. Who's the biggest of ya?" shouted the driver, surveying the group with narrow eyes for the first time. "You three up at the back. Come on, you seem to have the most energy, grab a shovel and clear that road."

Jack, Freddy and Knievel reluctantly reached behind the back seats and retrieved their thick coats, yanking their woollen beanie hats from the pockets. They made their way down the black rubber matting that ran down the aisle of the bus, and the bus door opened with a pneumatic hiss. The blizzard outside was so fierce that the boys could barely tell if it was day or night. They clambered out, taking a shovel each from Bob the driver as they left.

In the light of the headlamps, the children dug furiously, slinging heavy shovelfuls of wet snow onto the verge. Ten minutes later they banged on the minibus door and climbed back in, shaking snow all over the warm interior like dogs. As he walked past, Freddy slapped his ice-cold hands around Lance's face, grinning as he did so. Lance lurched his head back.

The bus pulled forward and slowly continued its ascent up the twisting gravel road. The snow was falling so thickly that Lance could only just make out the shadowy darkness of the trees that lined the road. When the forest broke to make way for a frozen lake, it felt like the bus was floating in space, with just white in every direction. Bob drove slowly, sitting upright in his chair, and focused intently on the road immediately in front of the bonnet.

After a nerve-racking thirty minutes, Bob called out, "There it is!"

A light on the gates of Fort Lagrave pierced through the grey fog, and they could roughly make out the shape of a long wall across the horizon. It had taken them six hours, and the time was now 2 PM, although it felt like night. Just as the group breathed a sigh of relief at arriving, the bus skidded on a patch of ice and slid sideways into the verge with a bang. The engine shrieked as Bob tried the accelerator, finding no grip and only wheelspin.

"Damn thing. I told the school to buy a four-wheel drive," he muttered, smacking on the steering wheel. "Everybody out!" he shouted back, and all six kids stood up and dug their thick coats from their bags, pulling on their gloves and hats. They all hustled outside the vehicle, where the snow was so heavy they could barely make out the gates of the manor house, despite it being only a few hundred metres away.

The bus was at an angle, with the left-hand wheels in the ditch, which sloped away from the road. They shovelled and pawed the snow from under the wheels and around the wheel arches, then lined up across the back of the bus to push it forward. Despite their best efforts, it would not budge.

Bob put snow chains onto the front tyres to give it grip, but he found that only one set of chains worked – the other had a broken link, which meant it would not stay on the wheel. He punched the tyre with his thick mittened hands in frustration.

After twenty minutes of digging, pushing and cursing, Bob relented and told everyone to reboard the bus. He followed them in, blowing on his hands to bring life back into them as the children retook their seats.

"Right, I've got no choice but to walk up to the manor house and get help. You all wait here, you understand me?"

His gaze fixed on each of them in turn, and they nodded.

"No fighting. No leaving the bus. No trying to get her moving. Nothing. Just wait quietly. Especially you two." Freddy and Knievel caught his laser-like stare.

Bob slammed the door shut and trudged off into the blizzard and howling wind, wading through snow that came up to his knees. Within seconds, the group could barely even see his outline. The whiteout had swallowed him up, and all they could make out was a white star of the light above the gates, barely piercing through an impenetrable white fog.

Lance noticed that Victoria had been eyeing his Rubik's cube and he offered it to her. Victoria was tall for her year and had a centre parting in her dark brown hair, which she tucked behind her ears. She wore denim dungarees and thick boots made by a company called Kamik, who were local to Quebec. One thing Victoria liked about Matagami was the unpretentious fashion. The endless winter and two-hour drive to the nearest big town meant nobody was looking at what you wore, and that suited her just fine.

"Do you know how to solve it?" she asked.

"No," admitted Lance. "My mom gave it to me just before I got on this bus. I can do one layer only, so far. It has some colours missing."

Victoria eagerly took the cube and began to play with it. Snow was accumulating on the windscreen, gradually turning the interior of the van to darkness. Outside, the wind howled and snow came down so thick and fast that they could barely make out the trees to the sides of the roads, or the gates of the manor. Jack turned on the interior light and began to wonder how long Bob had been gone.

"Hey, brainiacs," he yelled from his seat midway through the vehicle. "What time did Bob leave? Any of you notice?"

Lance and Dyani shrugged, and Victoria guessed it was about forty minutes ago.

"It doesn't make sense," Freddy said. "Look, you can practically see the gates. Even in this snow, say ten minutes to the gates, then maybe fifteen more minutes to the house?"

Knievel nodded in agreement, but Jack added, "We can only see the front gate. It might be another mile to the house for all we know, and he's as old as my grandpa. Then they have to get their gear on, start a car, shovel off the road and stuff. Let's give him a full hour from when he left before we start worrying."

With a general agreement in the group, it was left to Victoria to keep an eye on the time and tell everyone when an hour had passed.

It passed, and by this point the interior of the car was cold and all the children had their coats on. The heating was cranked up to full, but with the engine only murmuring along at tickover, it was not enough to fight the ice building up on all the windows.

"That's an hour," said Victoria to the rest of the group.

Knievel abruptly stood up and marched to the door, kicking it to free it up and bursting out into the blizzard. He slammed the door shut and peered into the distance, unable to make out Bob's footprints as they had already filled up with snow. The kids inside jumped when his arm swept across the windscreen, clearing it momentarily from the snow that had accumulated to a thick blanket. A few minutes later, he returned up the steps into the vehicle.

"This is dumb," he exclaimed. "Bob is prob'ly wrapped up warm by the fire eating s'mores while we're here shivering our asses off. I'm going in. From out here you can see the gates, just about. Jack, Freddy, you coming?"

The two boys at the back of the bus shifted, looking at each other to decide what to do.

Jack smiled and shook his head sagely. Although the distance to the manor house looked achievable – half a mile at most – they knew it was bear country, and even kids in primary school were taught to never leave your vehicle in a blizzard. In a whiteout like this you could barely see your hands in front of you, and people had been known to get lost despite being just twenty-five metres from safety.

Logic like that did not come so easily to Knievel's partner in crime.

"Yeah, I'll come," said Freddy. "You chickens can freeze in here. I like me some chicken nuggets."

He flicked the fur-lined hood of his parka over his head and walked down the aisle to his friend, taking a moment to slap Lance in the back of the head as he went past.

"I think we should sound the horn and flash the headlights," Victoria said quietly to Dyani and Lance. Freddy overheard her and let go of the handle he was about to pull to release the door.

"Actually Knievel, I've got a better idea."

Freddy sat in the driver's seat and revved the engine excitedly. He pressed all the buttons and levers as he searched for the headlights, until finally Knievel wrestled him out of the seat and pulled back on the stalk to the right of the steering wheel. The main headlights of the vehicle flashed wildly towards the house, and the two boys fought over the horn like maniacs. The rest of the kids covered their ears at the din.

Through the snowhole in the windscreen, Lance could make out the white light which, if he recalled correctly, was on the gates to the manor. He wasn't sure if the house, which was set deep inside this vast brick perimeter wall, would be able to see their flashing lights, or if their efforts would be futile. He was certain the noise of the horn would not carry over the deafening wind.

After several minutes, the light in the distance went out momentarily, then came on again. Once more off and on, and Lance cried out, "It's flashing. They see us!"

Fifteen minutes later, they saw another headlight coming towards them and heard the reassuring rumble of an engine. A black snowmobile – like a massive, wide motorbike made for driving on snow – pulled up alongside the bus.

A giant climbed off it, swinging his tree-trunk legs off the vehicle and yanking the bus door handle with his massive mittens. He poked his head inside, covered with a fur hat and goggles that left only his mouth and grey moustache exposed. He looked like a walrus.

"You must be the kids from down south. What the hell are you doing out here? Where's your driver?"

His voice was gruff and gravelly, like he had rocks tumbling in his throat too deep to cough up.

The trio at the front were shy and looked back to Jack as their inevitable spokesman.

"We got stuck in the ditch, couldn't dig it out. He left to go up to the manor about an hour and a half ago."

The man nodded and grunted, "I'll take two of you back with me now, then I'll return with a trailer for the rest of you."

With that he swung his leg back onto the snowmobile and turned it around, facing back up towards the gates. Freddy and Knievel ran to the front of the bus and jumped down into the snow. They climbed onto the back of the snowmobile, holding on to a metal rack mounted on the back as it zoomed off through the snow. The big man returned as promised about ten minutes later, towing a big metal trailer on skis. The remaining four children piled the luggage into it and then climbed atop the bed of backpacks and cases. They held on for dear life as it skipped across the snow up the road to the gates.

A brick wall, too tall by far to see over, curved off into the distance. They were unable to see it now as the heavy snow meant they could only see twenty metres or so, but that wall was miles long and ran in a huge ring around the property.

The snowmobile paused at the gates, which surged even taller than the wall that flanked them to either side. The word 'Lagrave' was welded into them. Another character wrapped up in furs yanked one side of the metal gates open as they arrived and slammed it shut afterwards, climbing on board the snowmobile behind the Walrus.

Once inside the walls, the snowmobile continued driving up a featureless driveway that led uphill, and within a minute or so the children could see the vast manor house come into view through the storm. Dyani thumped Lance to get him to look up through the furry portal in front of his eyes.

To the children from a small town where even the tallest buildings were dwarfed by the trees, it looked nothing less than a castle. They all now peered through the foggy white haze at the outline of the turrets and warm yellow lights that shone from the windows, criss-crossed with lead like the ones in a church.

The snowmobile drew to a stop at the foot of eight stone steps, and the gatekeeper climbed them to heave open the wooden doors to the manor. Inside, Knievel and Freddy were waiting cockily. The group ferried the bags up to the entrance and slung them inside onto the dark wooden floorboards, until finally the last of them was in and the doors were closed behind them. Their ears had to readjust to the sudden silence after the deafening din of the storm outside.

The snowmobile driver flicked back his hood and put his goggles onto his forehead. He was a tall man, aged somewhere between the children's parents and grandparents. His skin was wrinkled and leathery from years of working in hostile weather up here, and his cheeks were red with tiny veins you could only see when he was close. His teeth were bad and the whites of his eyes were bloodshot. He was clearly unused to children and mumbled short sentences with no pleases or thankyous.

"This is Fort Lagrave. Built 1752," he mumbled. "Mrs Duquette will see that you are settled in, and I must first see to your driver. He's likely gone into a side entrance." With that, he marched off down a long corridor to the right of the hallway. Lance noticed he had a rifle slung across his back.

The gatekeeper took off her coat and hat, and her brown plait fell down onto her back. As she shed her bulky parka, she halved in size to reveal a petite woman with mousy brown hair. She wore a blue dress, which had been repaired several times, and now she slipped on some flat white leather shoes. She put an apron over her neck and tied the long white ribbons around her waist. She reminded Lance immediately of his mother, and that made him breathe a comforting sigh of relief.

"Put your boots here, kids, under that bench, and your coats on those hooks. Then I'll take you to your rooms," she said warmly. "You must be freezing," she added, putting the back of her hand gently onto Lance's face to confirm.

"I'm Mrs Duquette, by the way. That was Mr Lagrave. Sorry, I should have introduced us. We're not used to company."

Meanwhile, Mr Lagrave left the side door in the east wing, returning to the storm.

"Anybody out there?" he called, cupping his hands to his mouth. The wind drowned his words, and he shook his head in irritation. Head down and hood up, he walked around to the front steps and disconnected the trailer from the snowmobile. He revved it into life and rode it to the gates, where he dismounted and peered through them.

"Is anybody out there?" he shouted.

He yanked the huge fur mitten from his right hand and reached into his jacket pocket for a metal key, with which he opened the gates. He pulled the gun from his shoulder and unclicked the safety so it was ready to fire if necessary. He walked slowly through the snow, scanning left and right with wide eyes and periodically stealing a glance down at the ground. He could see no footprints and was bewildered as to where the driver had disappeared to.

Then something dark caught his eye in the snow under a couple of tall pine trees. Startled, he raised his gun to his shoulder, but he saw that it was too small for a bear. Remains of a deer or moose, he assumed as he walked cautiously towards it. As he got closer, he saw it was the body of a human, with a leg completely missing. Knowing only one bear could have caused such massive, effortless damage, he swung his gun around in a full circle in anticipation of seeing the animal defend its catch.

He backed away from the corpse and returned to the gates, cursing into the wind and shaking his head with anger. He retrieved his snowmobile and drove out to the body, checking constantly to the left and right. He dragged the heavy torso onto the back of the sled and rode back towards the house, leaving a trail of blood in the snow. Inside the safety of the wall, he relocked the gates and dragged the body into a black barn in front of the house. He left it slumped on the concrete floor and roared with anger, punching the wall of the building. His swearing and screaming was swallowed by the howling wind, and he kicked open the side door to Fort Lagrave and returned inside the house.

Chapter 3

Fort Lagrave

The main entrance to Fort Lagrave was magnificent, with a double-height ceiling and a huge chandelier made of antlers hanging by a black chain from the rafters high above. At the back of the hallway a set of stairs ascended and split into two, curving back on themselves like ram's horns to become a gallery that overlooked the atrium. On the walls were old paintings of men, holding guns and wearing red military jackets.

The group barely noticed any of that because their attention was transfixed by the huge stuffed polar bear standing on its back legs in a menacing pose. Its arms reached up as if to grab at the chandelier above, and its mouth gaped open to display rows of teeth as long as fingers. It was beautiful and terrifying, all at once.

"Chop chop," said Mrs Duquette, standing at the foot of the stairs.

The children quickly hung up their coats and jostled for their bags, convening at the base of the mighty staircase.

"Come on, you. What are you waiting for?" Mrs Duquette called to Lance, who was dithering by the bear.

"There's a case missing. My wooden case. It's got my paints in it. It must be outside."

"Well, you won't be painting tonight, and you can't go back out in that weather. Let's get it tomorrow," she said. Reluctant to make a fuss, Lance followed the others upstairs. He kept looking back to double check they weren't there, and he asked Victoria and Dyani if they had seen them when they unloaded the bus.

"Stop being a girl about it," said Knievel, coldly.

Mrs Duquette led them up the stairs and onto the balcony overlooking the hallway. From there, several doors led to bedrooms, and Freddy and Knievel called shotgun as soon as she mentioned that one of the rooms had its own bathroom.

"I ain't staying in a wigwam with Pocahontas and Leonardo da Vinci," Freddy said, slinging his bags into the room with Knievel in tow.

The others all stayed in a big dorm room at the front of the property, which had four bunk beds so they each got a whole one – Dyani, Victoria, Jack and

Lance. They were able to use one bunk for their belongings and one for sleeping on. Lance noticed they were all choosing to sleep up high, and he did the same.

The dorm room was dimly lit and smelled like a wardrobe that was only opened once a year to get the winter coats out. The floor, like in the rest of the house, was made of dark wooden floorboards with gaps big enough for drafts to come through. On each side of the room were two bunk beds, and between them was a black bear-fur rug, complete with the animal's head and paws. A log fire provided the warmth, and two dark wooden trunks with rusted metal corners completed the room. Victoria looked inside them and found spare blankets, which filled the air with dust as she billowed it onto her bed.

Mrs Duquette apologised, feeling nervously responsible for every aspect of the manor. "I'd open a window, but not this time of year. This room hasn't been used for as long as I can remember, so you might find the fire smokes a bit until it gets going.

"You all right in this room, with the boys?" she asked Victoria and Dyani. "I had meant for you two to be in the one with the bathroom, and put the men in here."

Victoria looked at Dyani and they both shrugged, unwilling to decamp and deal with the inevitable drama of turfing Knievel and Freddy out of their new digs.

"It's fine, thank you," said Victoria.

Mrs Duquette left the kids to relax while she prepared dinner. Dyani wanted to chat but could see that Lance needed to process his thoughts. Victoria was happy reading her book and Jack was sleeping, so Dyani lay on her bed and watched the fire crackle.

At 7:45 PM there was a knock at the door and Mrs Duquette led the children downstairs to a large dining room, which adjoined the hallway through a wide doorway. The ceiling was high and curved, and the walls had intricate wooden panelling and were painted dark blue up to head height, then white above. The floorboards were ancient and undulated slightly to show the natural paths of two centuries of steps. In the centre of the room was a long mahogany dining table that could have seated twenty people, Lance guessed. Tonight there were ten chairs around it, and the children took their seats. The crimson velvet dining chairs had worn smooth and shiny, blackened and slumped in the centre under the weight of the years.

On the floor in one corner of the room was a metal bucket into which a drip fell with perfect regularity. Lance followed the column of water up to the ceiling, where blackened wooden rafters were visible through a soggy hole in the plaster.

Freddy looked under his bowl, then under his seat. "Just looking for your paint set," he joked cruelly. Lance said nothing and wondered what was causing the hate inside of Freddy.

The double doors leading to the kitchen swung open and Mrs Duquette brought out a tray of plates, each one with a bowl of stew and some bread.

"Moose pot roast," she announced.

"Thanks," said Victoria and Lance. Freddy and Knievel rolled their eyes. They had been crossing their fingers for cheeseburgers or chicken-fried steak. Despite having been born and raised in smalltown Canada, Freddy in particular liked to think of himself as a trendy Californian who was much too cool to live out here where the roads ended. Freddy liked to complain loudly about everything, from having to learn French to how backwards their classmates were – ironic considering he and Knievel were the true Neanderthals of the school.

Mrs Duquette ferried the remaining plates of stew. Here in Eastmain, as in the group's hometown of Matagami, moose were abundant. The group were all very used to eating caribou or moose stew, and Mrs Duquette's version was beautifully prepared.

Dyani's family, in particular, lived off the land in much the same way they had done for generations. Her mother and father were both accomplished trappers, leaving her and her sister with their grandparents for days at a time when they went gathering furs in winter and shooting geese in summer.

"This looks delicious," said Jack, who seemed as at ease with adults as he was with his own peers. "Mrs Duquette, we haven't seen Bob, our driver, since we arrived outside. Is he okay? Is he joining us?"

"Let me check," she said

Mrs Duquette knocked ever so gently on the door of the library.

"Enter!" Mr Lagrave called from within.

She slipped into the room and closed the door behind her. Lagrave was sitting on an armchair facing out of the rear windows of the property. He did not turn around, and she spoke to the back of his head.

"The children are asking where their driver is," she said nervously.

"Gone," he said simply, pouring himself a glass of whisky.

"What do you mean, sir? Gone home, in this weather? Did he get the bus out?" she asked anxiously.

"The bear took him."

She gasped and staggered back to lean on the closed library door. Regaining her composure, she walked to a chair. He stood and turned to face her.

"May I…" she asked, pointing to a chair.

He nodded, and she sat, while he paced along the windows looking out of the back of the property. She lifted her apron and wiped a bead of sweat from her forehead. She felt lightheaded and thought she might faint. As the realisation sank in, her anxiety drifted to her stomach and she felt sick with dread.

"Have you called the sheriff?" she asked.

"No. And we won't be doing so. He's gone, nothing any sheriff can do about it."

She looked up at him with a broken expression, unable to form words. Just hours ago she had felt like Fort Lagrave was at a turning point, and the sound of children's voices had warmed her heart for the first time in years. As she had retrieved more than two plates for dinner, she smiled and thought that finally a different future was coming. Now she felt numb, as she had become so used to over the years.

Lagrave continued, unprompted.

"If the police see that body, they'll find the bear that done it and shoot him dead. No bear, no tourists, no money."

He poured himself another whisky. Now that he had said it out loud, he became more committed to his plan.

"No bear, no tourists, no money."

He looked her right in the eyes as if to print a new truth permanently in her mind, and in his own.

"The driver left shortly after they arrived, in my vehicle. He wanted to get back and didn't want to disturb the children by saying goodbye. Is that clear?"

Her breathing was light and quick, and she looked down into her lap, adjusting her apron and smoothing it flat. Her fingers shook.

"Is that clear?" he repeated, slowly and with menace.

She nodded. Her throat was so dry and tight that it hurt to swallow.

"If I may," she whispered. "When he doesn't make it home tonight, what will his family say?"

Lagrave grunted and slumped into the tatty armchair, pulling off his heavy snow boots to reveal socks with holes in. He thought for a moment before brushing off her concerns like the snow from his boots.

"They'll assume he stayed the night, and that he'll come back another day. Maybe stayed the whole week. I don't know. Now, I'll be taking my dinner in here tonight. That will be all."

Mrs Duquette froze for a second too long as she tried to compute the various outcomes of this bombshell.

"That will be all!" he said angrily, his voice louder this time. "Damn, woman, must I repeat everything?"

She scuttled out of the library and paused in the hallway to check herself in the mirror. She breathed out slowly to stop herself from shaking and forced her face into a smile.

The group of kids paused their chatter when Mrs Duquette walked back into the dining room. She managed to speak confidently, despite her inner turmoil, and cleared the plates as she explained.

"Your driver wanted to make a break for it while the storm let up and left soon after he arrived. He had come in the side entrance while we were out looking for you. Mr Lagrave loaned him a four-wheel-drive car. He said to say goodbye and that he'd see you in a week. Now, I'll go fix dessert."

The group nodded and went back to their small talk. Mrs Duquette went into the kitchen and opened up three tins of peaches. A tear rolled down her cheek and dripped into the sugary liquid.

By the time dinner was over it was nearly 9 PM and the exhausted kids went upstairs to bed. Mrs Duquette brought a basket of firewood to the two bedrooms and explained that there was no central heating and if they let the fire die, the room would be cold by dawn. She put a stack of logs by the side of the hearth. After she left, Victoria considered organising a rota for feeding the fire, but she felt too lazy to wake up in the night and get out of bed.

The fire cast a warm glow over the rug, and Victoria left a table lamp on so that she could read. Lance was somewhat relieved, and he too read his book in the dim light. The four kids were on the top bunks of their beds, which creaked worryingly when they climbed the ladders or even rolled over. They could just about make out each other's faces as they looked across the room in the soft glow. The window rattled when the wind blew.

Dyani whispered to anyone that was listening: "What do you think we're going to do all week? I mean, it's like they've never seen a kid before. By the way, I can't believe Freddy and Knievel snatched our room."

"I know. I was like, eww. No offence, Lance," Victoria said.

"What about me? I can be offended too!" Jack snickered, turning his head on his pillow to face the girls on the other side. "It's weird, ain't it? My folks did warn me it was their first time hosting people. They wrote the school and said they had polar bears and could host six kids. Forty bucks a person. Luckily that's all my folks needed to know. Cheaper than feeding me at home was all they said, and signed me up!"

The others laughed. Jack had grown rather suddenly in his thirteenth year, re-emerging from the summer break more man than boy. He was now captain of the under-fifteens hockey team for the school. He seemed to Lance like he was from another generation, despite being just eighteen months older.

"This place is bleak," said Dyani. "And creepy."

"Matagami is bleak and creepy!" joked Victoria. "At least we get to miss a week of school."

The others laughed, except Lance, who slid his book into the gap between the mattress and the bed frame and closed his eyes to sleep. He wished he were home in his own bed and was already counting down the days to get out of this place. It was creepy indeed, and Freddy and Knievel were just stand-in menaces while he was out of his older brothers' punching range. At least, he thought, Dyani was so sweet. He went to sleep wondering why he'd had to get two brothers and no   sisters.

Chapter 4

Chandelier

Lance woke early with no idea what time it was. The fire had died and the room was cold enough that he could see his breath when he exhaled. He climbed out of his bunk very slowly to avoid it creaking and crept to the heavy red velvet curtains. He peered through a tiny crack in the curtains, cautious not to make the room light.

Outside there was enough dawn light to see the grounds of Fort Lagrave sprawling out before him. A heavy white blanket of snow stretched out from the stone steps to the boundary wall. From the house it was difficult to tell how tall it was, because the base of the wall was buried under a snow drift that climbed against the grey brickwork. Beyond the gates he could see the huge pile of snow that was once their bus, now completely buried by the storm. Dotted inside the grounds were outbuildings such as barns and sheds, and several huge woodpiles. Several cars were strewn to the sides of the property, in various states of disrepair, and there were lean-to shacks that looked like they housed machinery. Inside the boundary wall there were only a few trees, and beyond the wall it was a patchwork of iced-over lakes, and rocky snowfields, and forest.

Lance heard a noise and his attention snapped to the area below his window, where there was a black wooden barn. There, among dirty, muddy footprints, he saw the barn door open and Mr Lagrave back out of the building with a wooden wheelbarrow, loaded with a black plastic sack. He did a three-point turn and pushed the barrow along the pathway that led around the house, where he went out of sight.

"See anything interesting?" said Dyani, propping her head up onto her hands. It made Lance jump.

"Not really. Just white. Lots of white."

"Any bears?" she asked hopefully.

"Not yet. You can see our bus is buried though. Nothing else to report. I'm going to get a shower."

Lance wore blue-and-white pyjamas that reminded him of his old life in Ottawa, because they were from a department store called La Baie. He slung his bath towel over his shoulder and prepared a pile of clothes on his bed, including a pair of trousers, shirt, clean socks and underwear, and his toothbrush and toothpaste. Supporting the neat stack like a forklift truck, he opened the bedroom door and walked around the gallery to the communal bathroom.

The atrium was quiet and gloomy, and he wondered if it was too early to be taking a shower. He peered over the banister and looked down at the grandfather clock, which ticked loudly, just out of sync with a bucket collecting water by the front door. It was just after 7 o'clock, which Lance felt was a reasonable time to be getting up. As he walked around the gallery and drank in the detail of the atrium, he felt some of its initial grandeur begin to fade. Cracks ran down the plaster from ceiling to floor, and diamond-shaped panes of glass in the leaded windows were cracked. Remarkably, though, it felt clean and there was not a cobweb in sight.

The bathroom had been crudely converted to accommodate large groups of visitors and had three shower cubicles separated by sheets of plywood. He placed his new clothes on the wooden bench and got undressed with a towel wrapped around him, adding his pyjamas neatly to the pile. Inside the cubicle, he hung his towel over the door.

The shower was freezing cold, and despite waiting for several minutes it remained so. He bravely lurched in and out of it, but he was unable to bear the icy water and gave up. Clutching his own shoulders and shivering, he turned to leave the cubicle but found his towel must have fallen from the door. He carefully opened it, checked the coast was clear and reached for it, but it was gone. The bench, too, was empty. He double checked the hook inside the cubicle door, though he remembered he had definitely put all his stuff on the bench outside. He shook his head, knowing full well what had happened. Freezing cold and dripping wet, he crossed the bathroom, doing his best to cover himself up with his hands. He opened the door to the bathroom and looked across the hallway. Knievel and Freddy laughed like hyenas as Lance darted naked from the bathroom to his bedroom door, scrambling up the wooden ladder and diving under the covers of his bed.

"Whoa! What happened to you?" Victoria laughed.

"Freddy's doing, I'm guessing?" asked Dyani, to which Lance nodded. Jack reached into Lance's case and tossed him a handful of clothes, and Lance dressed himself under the covers.

The gang left their bedroom to discover Lance's clothes dangling from the chandelier that hung over the great hallway. His pants had even fallen through and landed on the polar bear's massive paw, much to everyone's amusement.

"You have to admit, it's quite funny. For them," said Victoria. Jack slapped Lance on the back and shook his head. Lance seethed.

Their fun was short-lived when Mr Lagrave stormed into the hallway.

"What is the meaning of this?" he roared. "Get down here, all of you. NOW!"

The six kids scurried down the stairs and stood in the hallway. He grabbed Freddy's lapels with his hands as big as bear paws. "Is this yours? IS IT?" he screamed in the boy's face. Freddy was terrified and shook his head, looking across at Lance. The Walrus dropped him and stalked across to Lance with his hands behind his back.

"Is that your clothing?" he said.

"I just had a shower and..."

"It's a yes or no question, you fool. Is. It. Yours?"

"Yes," whispered Lance, looking down at the floor.

Without warning, Mr Lagrave punched the boy in the gut, causing him to double over in agony and collapse to the floor. The others gasped as Lance, winded, desperately reached for a breath. His stomach and ribs were in pain and tears rolled from his eyes. Mr Lagrave walked away down the corridor, and the children stood in silence, terrified to move. Mrs Duquette emerged and surveyed the scene in horror.

"Oh Lord alive!" she said, making a sign of the cross on her chest. She stooped down and said to the others, "Well, come on! Help him up!"

They carried the limping and stunned Lance to the breakfast table. Dyani sat next to him and told him to breathe deeply, to see if it felt like his ribs were broken. He said it did not.

Mrs Duquette went to a storeroom in the back of the house and returned with her arm threaded through a wooden stepladder. She told the kids to get the hallway cleaned up quickly. Knievel set the ladder up next to the polar bear statue, retrieving the underwear. He had to use a broom to reach up and remove the towel and other garments from the chandelier, and he was relieved to get it all down without seeing the Walrus again.

Mrs Duquette brought out toast and scrambled eggs, and the drama faded. After the meal, she led the group to a long room on the ground floor to the back of the hallway, which she described as the chapel. It was somewhere between a church and a conference room, reflecting the gradual evaporation of faith over the ten generations who had lived here. One stained-glass window remained, depicting a bearded man with a red shawl draped from his shoulder to his waist.

"Freddy would have had that," Victoria joked. Dyani shook her head as if to say 'too soon'.

Three rows of wooden pews remained, but at the front there was a projector screen where the lectern and altar might once have been. On the wall hung a massive map of Canada, and some rugs had been placed on the stone floor to soften it a little.

Lance appeared to have recovered from his earlier attack, but he felt a wave of anxiety wash over him as Mr Lagrave swept into the room. "Right, men. You came here to learn about *Ursus maritimus*, and that is what we shall do. But first, let me tell you about this house.

"Sit!" he commanded, as if they were dogs. The children hastily took their places on the wooden pews, in roughly the same layout as they had adopted on the bus.

He jabbed a stick towards a map of Canada, which looked ancient like everything else in the house. His lecture about polar bears somehow required him to start with his favourite topic: the creation of Fort Lagrave. To the children it was an isolated, decaying relic. To Lagrave, it was the Taj Mahal.

"This estate was built in 1830 when the French and British reached James Bay. Animals were slayed and fortunes were made. The Hudson's Bay Company – you know about that?"

Some murmurs of "yes" came from the nervous students. Being from Quebec, they were well aware of the company, which had a controversial history. Lagrave continued to tell his own version of events, in which his ancestors were heroic explorers who brought order to a land of tribal savagery. Dyani, in particular, had to bite her tongue during his distinctly one-sided account.

The reality was that, when the Europeans got to the land we now know as Canada, they plundered it for fish, timber and fur with the expertise of First Nations people who had lived there for two thousand years. In this region it was the Cree – Dyani's ancestors – who had hunted beavers for the settlers in return for metals and guns. Unsurprisingly it was the natives who got the raw end of the deal, along with the beaver of course. The Hudson's Bay Company was so successful at plundering that it came to dominate an area that covered half of the continent. James Bay was an important centre as it sat on the confluence of several huge rivers, which were the motorways of their day.

The Walrus concluded his story, in which his trailblazing ancestors won the war with nature and turned beavers into gold. He finally circled back to the subject of polar bears.

"One such fortune was spent building this manor house, with land that covers hundreds of acres bordering James Bay. It's the last part of Hudson Bay to freeze and the first to thaw, and during the summer months we get polar bears. Mostly the bears are over the western side of the bay, but we've had one or two over here for the last few years."

He turned off the light at the back of the room and fired up a projector, which lit up a crackled video on the white screen up front. A black-and-white video began of an Inuit constructing an igloo, block by block. It lasted for twenty minutes, during which Mr Lagrave left the room. When it ended, the screen went black and the projector's motor continued to whirr. Nobody dared turn it off, but they also worried that he might explode with rage if they left it running. They were grateful when he returned and changed the reel for a short documentary about polar bears. He stayed for this one. It showed a bear pouncing on a seal as it surfaced for air, grabbing its head in its huge jaws and dragging it from the water onto the surrounding ice. It ate the quarry before its heart had stopped beating, covering its white face in blood.

"Incredible animal," he said as he turned on the lights. "Now I will show you to the viewing turret from which you can see for miles. Follow me." The group snaked after him through the labyrinth of rooms and corridors to a set of stone spiral stairs. They corkscrewed up and up until they reached a wooden doorway, which opened onto a small octagonal platform ringed with a crenelated wall. They were now above the height of the building's roof and able to see for miles across James Bay.

The wind was noisy here, and the kids had not worn outdoor clothes, so they turned up their collars and folded their arms to keep the cold out. The average temperature at this time of year was -5 degrees centigrade – colder than your fridge but not as cold as your freezer. With the wind blowing, bare skin would get frostbite in under thirty minutes.

"Out yonder, that's James Bay," shouted Lagrave. Lance peered out into the distance and could see miles and miles of snow. It looked much the same as Lake Matagami did during winter, but on a scale so vast that you had to turn your head to see it all. No trees, no colour - just a vast white sheet, as if the world had been erased.

A pair of binoculars hung from a hook, and Lagrave picked them up and peered out.

"There he is. The king of them all. You see?" The kids huddled in the cold air, desperate to return into the house but also eager to be next with the binoculars. Lance was the last in line, and in the distance he watched a lumbering mass of bear, padding across the snow. Even at this great distance he could tell it was a huge animal.

Mr Lagrave cracked a rare smile.

"That is the biggest bear in the world. When you get back, you tell people you saw it. The king of them all. You are lucky you only had to drive for five hours. People will come from New York City to see my bear."

The kids nodded diligently, shivering with cold as Mr Lagrave looked again through the binoculars, transfixed on the great white bear. Without warning, the Walrus shoved his binoculars into Jack's chest and disappeared down the stone stairs. The lesson, it appeared, was over. The group retraced their steps to the atrium and then up to their bedrooms. They wrapped themselves in blankets and warmed up by the fire.

Lance looked out of his window once more at the black barn he had been watching earlier. He wondered what Mr Lagrave did with the sacks of rubbish he'd carted around the back of the building. After all, it's not as if rubbish could be collected here. He must be burning it, he thought.

Chapter 5

The Shovel

The group was unsure what to do with themselves. They would have loved to explore the manor house, with its spiral stairs and countless nooks to hide in. However, Mr Lagrave's reaction to the prank Freddy had played made them hide in their rooms when they weren't eating a meal in the dining room. They had come to use the larger dorm room to relax in, where they would chat and play cards.

At lunch, Knievel asked Mrs Duquette if they could play outside.

"Of course!" she said. "You be sure to wrap up warm, though."

Lance guarded the outside of the dorm room door as Dyani and Victoria got changed, layering on all the clothes they had. Victoria emerged, joking that she now felt like the great fat bear they had seen from the turret.

The group went out into the grounds, which were protected from the dangers beyond by the high wall. Lance, Victoria and Dyani hung out together, walking a lap around the house, which took forty minutes. Jack, Knievel and Freddy had found a log in lieu of a football, and they tossed it to each other in a wide triangle.

After some time, the group converged around the west side of the house, where fuel was prepared for the fire. Wood was stacked up against the side of the house, five logs deep. Above it, a corrugated iron roof protected them from the worst of the weather and protruded far enough to enable Dyani to hide from the flurries of snow. The others sat on stumps, which were dotted among a carpet of wood chips. Freddy found an axe and raised it above his head, motioning to throw it at Lance and then erupting in laughter when his victim inevitably jumped.

As soon as they stopped playing, even the thickest gloves and coats could not stave off the bitter cold. Knievel suggested they build a maze out of tunnels in the snow, which they all agreed to. They gathered up all the snow shovels they could find from around the property, of which there were several. Starting near the front steps, they began to excavate tunnels through the deep snow. Doing so was banned at school because there was a risk of the roof falling in and suffocating the children within. Although it carried a risk of death, today it felt like the safe option as they could remain out of sight of the Walrus, as they had come to describe him.

Lance sat down in a tunnel he had built, panting and exhausted by the effort. The hole he had dug was tall enough to walk through in a crouch and wide enough that his elbows could touch both sides at once. The ceiling was about as thick as a school ruler but dotted with holes where the snow had collapsed during its construction. As a result, light pierced through in patches, but it still felt subterranean. Dyani was impressed when she broke through from hers to his. The one she had dug was more of a trench, so she was impressed that Lance had managed to keep the ceiling intact.

In that moment, looking down his snow tunnel, Lance smiled. Against his expectations, he had made friends and was playing in the group like a normal kid. He remembered the injustice of being punched in the gut that morning by Lagrave and tried to put it behind him. When I'm old, I won't still be mad at him, he reasoned. If I'm going to let go of the anger at some point in my life, I might as well do it sooner than later. He had used this technique before to forgive his brothers and father. "Anger can fill you up," his mother would warn.

Jack came scrambling into the tunnel and hid with Lance, raising his finger to his lips and mouthing "Shhh". In the distance, Freddy called, "Jack!", and the two boys hiding in the tunnel tried not to laugh.

They played all afternoon until their network of tunnels was trashed and most of the ceilings had caved in. As the sky darkened from one shade of grey to another, the girls went in and only the boys remained outside. Jack, Knievel and Freddy tossed a log around the woodcutting area at the other side of the house.

Lance was sitting in the end of a tunnel, exhausted from playing and getting ready to head back indoors, when the still air was broken by a metal door slamming. He instinctively looked towards the noise, his head rising over the surface of the snow, and saw he was near the black barn he had seen from his bedroom window.

Terrified of bumping into the Walrus, he dropped down beneath the surface like a mouse might escape a hawk. He sat in that hole for several minutes, unable to resist peeking periodically above the surface, where he saw Mr Lagrave emerge with a wheelbarrow. In it was another black plastic rubbish sack. A path had been cut into the snow around the footprint of the house, running from the black barn towards the back of the property, and having sat there for a while Lance could see that the Walrus was ferrying something away from the black barn.

Despite the risks, the young boy's curiosity drew him to the barn. When the Walrus was walking away and had gone up the path, Lance gingerly emerged from the snowy hole and crept along the edge of the barn. Convinced Lagrave was long gone, he decided to run along the path in front of the barn doors so that if he was caught, he could play it off as if he were playing an innocent game. Jogging through the deep snow, he glanced into the barn and saw a thick trail of blood on the concrete floor of the barn, and what looked like a glove. As his sight fixed on it for a second, he thought it looked like a human hand.

Lance continued to run, fast now, and as he rounded a corner of Fort Lagrave he felt a shovel hit him square in the face. The metallic clang rang through his brain and his vision blacked out.

He lay on the snow, face up. Blood streamed from his nose and his ears were ringing. His eyes saw flashes of purple, and through them he saw the grizzled face of the Walrus, holding a snow shovel as if ready to decapitate the boy with it.

"What are you doing!" the great ogre screamed. "I might have known it would be you again, ya little runt."

Lagrave dropped to his knees and lurched towards the boy, wrapping his thick mittens around his throat.

"What did you see?" he raged, his eyes wide and bloodshot and breath stinking of whisky.

"Nothing!" Lance gasped, grabbing the wrists around his neck and trying to prise them off. "I was just playing hide and seek with my friends."

The Walrus stared into Lance's eyes and watched his skin go dark red and almost purple. Lance felt the life drain from him and writhed helplessly under the weight of the beast.

"Then you tell them you saw nothing. Because if you tell them anything else" – he moved his face so close their noses almost touched – "I'll kill you."

The Walrus released his strong fingers and Lance gasped for breath. With his head half buried in the snow, he looked up at the flashing purple sky, tasting the trickle of blood that ran from his nose to his lips and tickled his neck as it dripped to the ground. By the time he fully came round and sat up, Mr Lagrave was long gone and the black barn door was closed. As he regained his senses, Lance climbed to his feet and walked into the house with his chin up, pinching his nose shut and peering down through the gap between his fingers.

Lance kicked off his boots in the hallway and fought off his parka with only one hand at a time. Upstairs in his bedroom, he found Dyani reading.

"Whoa!" she said, dashing out to the bathroom and returning moments later with a toilet roll and a metal waste-paper basket. "What happened?"

"He hit me. With a shovel," replied Lance with a nasal voice.

"Who, Freddy?" Dyani asked.

"No, Lagrave," sighed Lance. "Again."

She mopped up his face with a wad of toilet roll that Victoria had unravelled on his lap.

"Let me look at it," she said.

Lance reluctantly moved his fingers away from his nose and Dyani gently touched it, running her finger down the bridge from top to bottom. She very gently pinched it to feel if it was straight.

"It's not broken by the looks of things. Why did he do it?"

"He thought I saw something in the black barn," Lance said.

Jack knocked gently and came in, closing the door quietly behind him.

"Mrs Duquette is looking for you. Says she heard about what happened and wants to check you're all right," he said, before returning to Freddy and Knievel's room.

"You saw something in the black barn. What did you see, Lance?" Victoria asked. Her dark brown hair was wet, and she squeezed the moisture out with her towel.

"Nothing. I didn't see anything. I don't know why he did it."

"Well, he must have thought you saw something in there if he hit you with a shovel," she said suspiciously.

Mrs Duquette whirled in with a copper bowl full of soapy water. By this point the blood had stopped flowing, and she looked nonplussed when she saw Lance's red-stained jaw. She said simply, "Let's get you cleaned up," and set the water and some cloths on the bedside table. As Dyani and Victoria looked on from the other side of the room, she dipped a white handkerchief into the suds and gently wiped the blood from Lance's lower face.

"He thought you were a bear. That's what happened. He didn't mean any harm. He's a good man, Mr Lagrave."

She tossed the filthy cloths into the wastebasket and scooped that up in one hand and the water bowl in the other.

"You lot put something smart on for dinner please, at eight o'clock sharp," she said. "Mr Lagrave will be joining you."

"Are you okay?" Lance said to Mrs Duquette as she was leaving the bedroom. She looked back at him, surprised to hear someone asking about her wellbeing.

"Me? Yes dear, I'm fine. Why?"

"It's just, you're limping slightly and I didn't notice that before."

She looked down at her leg and forced a smile, taking care to walk naturally as she left the room.

The kids were down at dinner several minutes early, tucking napkins into the necks of their white school shirts, which would have to last them all six nights. They sat in silence while Mrs Duquette scurried around them like nothing was wrong, and they felt the hairs on their necks rise up when Mr Lagrave strode in carrying a green bottle of gin. He sat at the head of the enormous table and tucked a napkin into his shirt.

"I trust you're all having a pleasant week? Or weekend," he said, looking at his wrist for a watch that wasn't there. "What day is it?"

The children glanced at each other, none wanting to engage in conversation with the monster.

"Sunday," said Jack finally.

The Walrus poured himself a glass of neat gin and sipped it, mumbling on.

"Ah, Sunday. You lose track of time here. But you must have routine. You must maintain certain standards. Sunday means venison and dauphinoise potatoes. I trust that is to your satisfaction," he said with a menacing grin.

The group nodded politely, and Mrs Duquette came through the double doors from the kitchen, which hinged both ways like in a Wild West saloon. She carried a plate of food and delivered it to Mr Lagrave, nervously standing to the side as he leaned in towards it and inspected the meal.

"Jelly," he grunted.

"Oh, I'm sorry sir. I'll fetch the cranberry jelly," she said, darting off to the kitchen.

Lagrave shook his head, then made a sickly smile as he recognised Lance, whose nose and eye socket were bruised.

"I thought you were a wild beast, tearing around the corner like that. You need to be more careful, boy. I've got the killer instinct, you see. You know what they say, 'You can take the man out of the army but you can't take the army out of the man.'"

Lance forced his lips straight. It wasn't a smile, but it was as much as he could muster for the poisonous monster who had assaulted him twice in one day. He was grateful when his food arrived and the spotlight of attention shifted away from him.

Their dinner was delicious, with neatly sliced venison, seared on the outside and just pink in the middle. The potatoes were thinly sliced and baked in a rich cream sauce. Alongside was steamed okra. Mrs Duquette did not join them for the meal.

The conversation turned to polar bears, and to how magnificent 'his' bear was.

"Have you ever seen something so mighty?" he asked. "No, nobody has. Not in this world or the last." Victoria and Lance caught each other's confused looks.

The Walrus unscrewed the gin bottle and poured some over the ice in his tumbler. The light from the candelabra on the table shone through the green glass and projected a blur onto the dark wall of the dining room. His shaky pour was amplified in the green silhouette, which swung back and forth over the painting of his ancestor. Lance imagined the old colonel in the painting would turn in his grave if he could see his monstrous descendent drowning him in gin.

The Walrus drank and refilled constantly, tearing at his dinner like an animal. He reminded the children yet again that one day people would travel (from New Orleans, this time) to see the world's largest polar bear. He would make his ancestors proud by restoring Fort Lagrave to its original glory, he said, convincing nobody but himself. Meanwhile, the water dripped through the hole in the ceiling into the bucket in the corner.

"This place was built on the money from fur. So it will be once again. The road is there, and now people will come to see my bear. Busloads and busloads... of money."

After dinner they returned to their bedrooms and looked out of the window. Snow was falling again, and by the time they went to bed it was heavy enough to have made their maze disappear. They had five more days of being trapped with this maniac.

Chapter 6

Gunshot

Lance was woken in the middle of the night by a gunshot, which felt so deafeningly close that, in that hazy moment when he was transitioning from asleep to awake, he thought he'd been shot. All four children in the dorm room climbed down from their bunks and ran into the gallery to see what was going on. They felt the cold air hit them immediately. Knievel soon joined them, as did Freddy, who had darted out of his bedroom in only his underwear. The wind howled in through the double doors, which were open to the night. Snowflakes blew into the hallway, reaching all the way to the yellowing fur of the stuffed polar bear.

The Walrus stood in the hallway with one hand holding the butt of his gun and the smoking barrel resting on his shoulder. He was dressed as he had been for dinner last night, but with his shirt now untucked and a trapper hat on.

"Get out here NOW!" he spat.

The group lined up on the gallery in their pyjamas, shaking with cold. He stared up at them, looking every bit as menacing as the stuffed polar bear to his side.

Satisfied everyone was there, including Mrs Duquette who stood in her nightgown in the dining room doorway, he slammed the front doors shut with a bang.

"This house is a disgrace! Your mess all over it, and I'm not having it."

Six pairs of boots were neatly lined up under a wooden bench in the hallway, and he swung his foot at them and scattered them across the floor, as if to prove his point.

"My ancestors. Look at them!" he screamed, waving the barrel of his gun towards the massive painting of Pierre-Luc Lagrave that hung on the wall at the top of the stairs. The children instinctively ducked as the muzzle of the gun swung across them.

"My forefathers did not pour their lives into this building to have it treated like a nest by feral city children. Tomorrow at 6 AM you will be UP, and you will be on your knees scrubbing this place until it shines. Am I clear?"

The group nodded. He waved his massive gun round to Mrs Duquette, who gasped in fright as the barrel pointed at her face.

"Am I clear?" he bellowed.

"Yes, sir," she said fearfully, and he swung the barrel back onto his shoulder.

"I will see you at breakfast," he said, picking up an uncorked bottle of red wine from the foot of the polar bear statue, tripping over the boots he had kicked around the hallway as he staggered back towards his bedroom in the east wing.

The children went back to sleep, except Lance, who spent most of the night worrying he wouldn't wake up.

At 5:30 AM Mrs Duquette bustled into the dorm room, throwing open the curtain and clapping noisily.

"Up, up. Come on, you heard the man. I want you all downstairs in the hallway at five to six. You've got twenty-five minutes to get ready."

Lance climbed out of the creaky bed and carefully remade it, folding the corners neatly as his mother had taught him. Dawn would not break for another hour or two, and the house was dimly lit.

At the bottom of the stairs, Mrs Duquette waited with her trademark pale blue dress with white apron and a white hat covering her brown hair, tied up in a bun. Her face was gaunt, and she was thin from years of living in a state of constant fear. She carried a list, and as the children assembled she assigned them tasks, from polishing silverware to sweeping out the hearth.

They set to work, wondering how their week-long holiday had turned so quickly into a prison camp. Lance and Dyani were tasked with washing the wooden floorboards, which were already relatively clean. Still, they scrubbed until both arms ached and they had blisters on their fingers from the wooden brushes. Victoria was told to polish cutlery, and for hours she simply moved the already shining silverware from one box to another.

Freddy, Jack and Knievel, being the biggest of the bunch, were made to shovel snow outside in the blistering cold. Despite their thick gloves and hats, their hands were numb and the hours until the sun rose above the horizon felt endless. Finally, when the warm light spread across the grounds of Fort Lagrave, they realised they were being watched.

Freddy carried a shovel full of snow to a pile they had made to the side of the path and timed his trip to meet with Knievel. He sidled up to his friend, not slowing his work for even a second, and said, "Don't look up... but he's watching us from the turret."

They parted ways and continued to dig away at the endless snow drifts around the house. Once they had cleared the path that ran all the way around the house, they set to work on the driveway leading to the gates. At eight o'clock, the children were called inside for breakfast.

Sitting at the great dining table, the children reconvened and ate toast and honey, with some bacon. There was plenty of meat in the manor house kitchen but very few vegetables. In the short sub-Arctic summer, the days were long, and Mrs Duquette was able to grow plenty of turnips, radishes and cabbages during those couple of hot months. But the winter dragged on well into May, and nothing would grow when the ground was frozen solid. With no neighbours to trade with and hundreds of miles to the nearest city, the winter diet was rich in deer, moose and bear meat, but fruits were a delicacy only found in chutneys and jams preserved from the previous summer.

Mr Lagrave joined the kids for breakfast and ate quietly, not interested in conversation. He drank only coffee and seemed to even struggle with that.

"I've got them doing cleaning," Mrs Duquette reassured him as she filled his mug. "Will you be needing them after lunch?" she asked, nervously.

He grunted and shook his head.

"Nobody leaves the grounds," he said, tearing at a lump of bread.

"What do you do?" he said gruffly to Dyani, picking her at random.

"I was scrubbing the floor," she said meekly.

"I mean, what do you do for fun? You hunt? You fight? You're Indian, ain't ya?"

"Yes. James Bay Cree. I like to fish with my parents," she replied.

"Bet you do," the Walrus said. "No rules for you folk. Fish whatever you want."

Dyani said nothing, and he shifted his focus to Lance and grunted, crumbs of bread tumbling over his chin.

The shy boy swallowed, having no hobbies like hunting and fighting to fall back on. Much to his father's irritation, Lance's hobbies were limited to art, baking with his mum and writing stories.

"I paint," he said honestly.

The man squinted at him as if Lance had said he built space rockets.

"What do you mean, you paint? You paint houses?"

"No, I paint landscapes in acrylics."

The Walrus readjusted in his seat. "Like that?" he said incredulously, pointing at the portraits on the wall.

"Yes. Well, I'm not that good, but that sort of thing."

The oaf sat back in his chair and looked at the boy, slowly absorbing the idea that the skinny runt might have more uses than simply scrubbing the decks. He stood up and said, "Come with me. The rest of you, back to work."

"Did you see the sign at the highway when you were coming in?" the Walrus asked as he put on his boots.

Lance said yes and pulled on his coat and boots. He shuddered at the idea of going outside with him but was unable to avoid it.

"It says *Fort Lagrave*," the Walrus continued, pulling on his hat. "I want it to say *See the World's Largest Polar Bear* and have a painting of the Great White Bear. Can you paint that?"

"I can try, sir," he said. "But I don't have my paints. They must be in the bus."

"There's nothing in the bus," he said gruffly, opening the front door. "Follow me!"

Lance shadowed Mr Lagrave down the stone steps – snow free and freshly gritted by the other boys – to a shed around the back of the manor house. Like the barn out front, it was black and smelled of creosote, a nasty chemical used in those days to fend off rot. The snow had stopped, and although the sky was a flat grey, there was a patch of bright light where the morning sun tried to punch through.

They passed the spot where Lagrave had smashed him in the face with a shovel. He had spent the night tossing and turning, wondering if he would die out here in the wilderness and end up in a black bin liner in the barn. He had been forced further and further north, first by his dad and now by his school. Finally he was so deep in the white wilderness that the howling wind could extinguish his flame with a pinch of its fingers. His brothers would not miss him, and nor would his dad. But his mum would, and the thought of being back in their little kitchen, singing to the radio, gave him the fight he needed to get on with his day. She was the sunlight trying to fight through the clouds.

The shed door swung open. The inside was stuffed with bric-a-brac. Gardening tools leaned up in the corners, and shelves were lined with bottles of wood preserver and paint. Rat traps and a savage-looking bear trap hung from the ceiling, and bottles of poison filled a whole shelf, some bottles with orange warning labels with a skull. Everything one could need to fight off nature was here, and yet even this shed itself was inevitably losing the battle, its roof rotted through and rodent droppings everywhere.

The Walrus nodded towards a shelf at the side. "Paint," he said. Then he dug through a wooden box of screwdrivers and rusting tools and found a paintbrush, as wide as his massive bear-paw hand. He slung it to the ground, then backed up into Lance, who scurried out of the door.

"Well, don't just stand there, ya idiot!" he shouted, and Lance returned into the darkness of the shed to see Lagrave reaching up to the rafters and holding the end of a sheet of plywood.

The young boy climbed over lawnmowers and chainsaws, weaving between narrow gaps between old furniture, to get to the back of the shed to support the other end of the sheet of wood. He reached up but was too short to even make contact with the wood, let alone support it as it was heaved out.

"For God's sake!" the Walrus shouted angrily, yanking at the wood on his own. It slid towards him on the high horizontal rafter, and after a few steps back it pivoted to slope down towards him. On top of the sheet were other pieces of wood, which unexpectedly rained around him, and one timber beam slid down and hit him in the face. He staggered back and the whole sheet of plywood came crashing down, narrowly missing his feet.

Angry, frustrated and bleeding, Mr Lagrave leaned against the house and pulled out his metal flask. He unscrewed the lid and swigged it, wiping the blood from his face on the back of his plaid shirt.

Lance was stuck in the shed in almost darkness because the plywood had stuck at an angle, with one end on the ground and the other still in the rafters. He heard Mr Lagrave shout, "You got what you need now. Paint me a sign, boy. And get this place cleaned up."

The gruff voice trailed off and Lance found himself in the dark, trapped behind some wood. He eventually managed to extract himself from the shed and went inside to find some of the others to help. He got Jack, Dyani and Victoria to return to the shed with him and get the wood out. They tidied up the planks and offcuts that had fallen down, and carefully they threaded the longer timbers back into the rafters.

There were about ten dented tins of paint, intended for painting the walls of a house.

"Can you do it?" Victoria asked.

"Not really," Lance said. "I paint with oils and acrylics. This is just house paint. It dries much too fast, and we have barely any colours. Look at this – how am I meant to use this as a canvas?" he exclaimed, pointing at the warped sheet of plywood, which had turned brown with damp. "He's expecting me to paint a picture like the ones on the wall, and he'll end up hitting me when I can't do it."

"You're not going to like this brush either," said Victoria, holding up the enormous wooden brush with bristles dried rock hard with encrusted paint.

Lance sat on the floor, defeated before he had started. He was desperate to avoid the wrath of Mr Lagrave, but he felt it was inevitable.

Dyani began to take the paints down from the shelf, saying optimistically that there was lots of white and grey.

"Here." She passed a jam jar with miscellaneous nails to Jack. "I bet there's a hammer in that drawer. Let's knock up a stand to make the wood stay up straight while he's painting on it. What's it called?"

"Easel," said Lance.

Jack and Victoria held up some lengths of wood to make an A shape, and Dyani hammered in a nail at the top where they crossed. She did the same for another pair and then leaned the plywood up against it inside the shed, almost filling the outbuilding from one wall to the other. She found some old cast-iron clamps and tightened up the sheet of wood to the frame at chest height.

Then Victoria soaked the huge brush – designed for spreading paste onto wallpaper – in an ice cream container of white spirit, which instantly clouded. She cut some bristles from it and taped them to a screwdriver with some black electrical tape to make a smaller brush.

It was starting to look more doable, and Lance thanked his roommates for helping. He levered the lids from the dented tins of paint and found that most of them were dried up completely. A few had a thick, leathery skin on top, which he had to puncture with a screwdriver to get through to some liquid paint. He had plenty of white and grey to paint the polar bear, but he needed a dark colour for a background. He knew that if he painted a realistic scene, with a bear against the snow and a grey sky, it would look like a sheet of white to cars on the highway. The only dark colour the kids could find in the shed was the sludgy black paint that was used to tar the outbuildings.

"Well, at least it will protect it from the elements," said Dyani.

His helpers took turns to sit on furniture in the shed or wait outside and keep watch for Mr Lagrave. They knew that if he appeared they would have to look busy, as it was not yet lunchtime.

Lance sketched out the huge sheet of wood with a carpenter's pencil he found in a filing cabinet. He evenly spaced out the words *Fort Lagrave* along the top, each letter as tall as his hand, and then *See the World's Largest Polar Bear* along the bottom. In the middle would be the white shape of a massive bear, as wide as his outstretched arms.

"How can you just get that spacing right? You didn't even mark the middle of the wood, or anything.

If I'd have done that, I would have gotten to 'world's largest' and run out of room," said Jack, respectfully.

Lance painted the letters in the gloopy white paint, using the wide brush to stamp the straight parts in one go and finishing the curves of the lettering with the screwdriver brush Victoria had made. Then he filled in the outline of the massive white bear in brilliant white, then mixed up a little tar with the white paint to give it a gradient around the edges.

The bear had tiny black dots for eyes, a sharp head and a huge long neck that hung out like a crane. At least, that was how Lance remembered it looking when he had seen it from the turret the previous day. Once he had got the white parts done, he dipped the big brush into the tin of black paint, which smelt so strongly of chemicals it made his eyes water. Now he carefully filled in the rest of the sheet of wood in jet black, being sure to not let any paint run into his polar bear or lettering.

"Is it okay?" Lance asked nervously to the others, stepping back at last. "Is this what he wanted?"

The other three stood alongside him and admired the painting.

"I think it looks amazing, but who knows what he'll think," said Jack, patting Lance on the back.

They cleaned up the brushes as best they could with white spirit – leaving them in a much better state than they'd found them in – and returned to the house while the paint dried.

Lunch was smoked salmon with bread and capers, and Mr Lagrave did not join them. Nor did Mrs Duquette, and Lance wondered if she ever ate anything at all.

In the afternoon, the boys played outside in the snow and were grateful not to be watched by Mr Lagrave, who they assumed was sleeping off his hangover. Without the threat of the alpha bully, Freddy reassumed his position at the top of the food chain.

"Look at its stupid long neck," he said to Knievel, desperate to find fault with the new polar bear sign. "It looks like a giraffe!"

Later, during a game of football, Freddy pinned down Lance in the snow and said, "How's your new daddy?", referring to the seemingly preferential treatment Lance had received when he was led off to paint.

"Get off him," called Jack. "It ain't his fault he can actually *do* stuff beyond shovelling snow."

Over near the wall, so far from the house that there was no possible way Lagrave could hear them, the group congregated and discussed their predicament.

"Do you really think Bob the driver left on that first night we arrived?" asked Victoria. "I mean, that blizzard was heavy, and the road was so deep in snow we couldn't tell where the verge started. And why didn't he say goodbye to us?"

The kids kicked around the snow in the shadow of the high wall.

"Well, what else happened to him?" asked Freddy. "He ain't still here, unless he's dead, stoopid."

"How do we know he's not dead? The Walrus hit Lance in the face with a shovel. He punched him in the gut. He's a psycho!" said Victoria.

"Naa," said Knievel, shrugging off the suggestion. He had seen some strange and sometimes violent behaviour from his own father when he drank heavily. "He's a drunk, but he ain't a killer. I mean, why would he kill a bus driver literally the moment he stepped out of the bus? But then leave us all alive? It doesn't make sense."

The group seemed to roughly agree that it seemed unlikely the Walrus had attacked and murdered Bob and disposed of the body in the ninety minutes they'd waited in the bus that night. But they also found it hard to believe that their driver would have left the house without even saying goodbye or waiting till the storm had passed. Being stuck on James Bay Road as night fell would have been quite a scary drive.

Lance sat quietly and did not add to the conversation. He wanted to tell the group about the hand, but he couldn't shake the memory of Lagrave looming over him, threatening to kill him if he spoke up.

"Lance can just go ask him. Those two are tight now. He's your new dadda!" Freddy teased. "Lance and Walrus up a tree, K-I-S-S…"

The others groaned and shook their heads.

"Jeez, Freddy, what are you, six years old?" Jack said. "This is serious stuff. How do we get out of here? He's violent and this place is hell. I want to get out of here and don't want to wait another five days to get picked up."

They all nodded.

Victoria said, "We need to get to a phone, then ask our parents if Bob made it home. If he did, we tell them to send him right back and pick us up because we're having a terrible time. If he didn't make it back to Matagami, then they need to send the police because we're in a house with a murderer. So it's simple: send Bob, or send the cops."

"Have any of you seen a phone?" Dyani asked.

"We could ask Mrs Duquette?" suggested Knievel. "She might have a landline in the kitchen or something."

So with that agreed, they headed in, stopping at the shed to carry the sign, which was now dry. They brought it into the dining room and left it on the makeshift easel, nervously awaiting the Walrus's feedback.

Chapter 7

The Sign

The children dressed as neatly as they could manage, and when they convened for dinner they sat and tucked napkins into their collars. The huge black sign sat on the A-frame on one side of the room, parallel to the table. The white bear on it was massive – not quite life size but certainly as big as a yearling. Their chatter halted as they heard the heavy stomp of Lagrave's boots coming from the east wing. He had been grumpy at breakfast and asleep most of the day, so they were not sure what to expect.

The kids did a double take when they saw him saunter in wearing a top hat, transfixed on the sign and drawn towards it. He touched the coarse black surface and traced his finger around the head of the polar bear, feeling the ridge where the black paint met the white.

88

He moved his head just a hand's distance from the surface of the painting and looked at the fur on the bear, whose brushstrokes swept back realistically from its head towards its tail. There was even a shimmer of yellow in the bear's fur, which Lance had achieved by using some of the oil that had separated from the paint.

He stepped back and read it out loud word by word like a young child learning to string their first sentence together.

"Fort Lagrave. See the world's largest polar bear."

He turned and looked for Lance, stalking around the table with echoing footsteps that sent shivers up their spines. Standing behind Lance, he set his huge paws on the boy's shoulders, squeezed around his neck, and shook him forward and back.

"It's magnificent," he grunted. "The world's largest polar bear. You're damned right he is!"

Lance felt the weight lift from his shoulders in every sense when the Walrus went to his seat and inspected the bottle of red wine that Mrs Duquette had placed next to his glass. He filled it and raised a toast.

"To the world's largest polar bear!" he said, swilling back the wine and quickly refilling it. Following Victoria's lead, the kids lifted their glasses of water and repeated his toast.

By the time the main course of roasted grouse had appeared, he had finished the first bottle of wine and moved onto whisky. His face reddened and he kept inserting his finger around his collar as he sweated. He was a different man to the one who had kicked open the front door at 1 AM and rung gunshots into the night air. The excess of alcohol had put him in a buoyant mood.

Noticing Dyani looking at the painting on the wall, he said, "That's Jean-Luc Lagrave. Second generation Lagrave. Fine man. I will tell you the story of how he built this place, as it was told to me."

He set his hat on the table and began grunting the story of his great ancestors and the creation of Fort Lagrave. His eyes bulged so wide as he leaned into the table that Lance couldn't help but examine the web of thin red lines that bifurcated like rivers over the yellowing whites.

"Once the Europeans arrived in the 1600s – in their thousands – they set about fishing. It didn't take them long to discover great fish stocks out on the Grand Banks, off the coast of Newfoundland. It was teaming with cod. You could reach your hand in and pull one out of the water. These settlers harvested cod in the millions, dried it and shipped it back across the Atlantic to Europe. Now, the journey across the Atlantic was cold and took months, so before they left, these cod fishermen traded with the natives for beaver pelts to keep them warm for the journey. Your kind."

He pointed a menacing fat finger at Dyani and paused to swig his whisky. He was more animated tonight than he had been before, and he looked around at the kids as he spoke. They listened hard to pick out the individual words from his gravelly monologue.

"Well, in France, the hat makers were very pleased when they saw these fishermen arrive in beaver robes. Because beaver felt makes a fine hat. So much so that the European beaver had been hunted to extinction. Now it don't look like beaver fur when they're done with it. It gets turned into felt and made into any shape. Top hats, army hats, pirate hats. This hat – all made of beaver fur. This hat is 200 years old and looks like it was made yesterday."

He passed the hat to Victoria, who had been shoved back when the boys raced to get the seats furthest from the Walrus. The hat smelled musty and ancient, but she nodded politely and passed it around the table.

"The fur they were wearing for the journey, well, that was worth more than the fish in the hold. So the French and British fishermen dropped their nets and came inland by river and creek to seek out tribes who could find more beaver. See, they couldn't catch the animals themselves. They'd bring iron and rum, and the natives would go out and strip the rivers. Quebec was built on the money from beaver fur."

The children were gripped by his story, and for a moment they forgot how terrifying he could be. When he talked about the glory days of Fort Lagrave and his ancestors, he came alive. He swigged his whisky enthusiastically and rumbled through the story he had told many times.

"But with money comes blood. The natives began to fight each other for the land that might still have some precious beaver. My ancestors, seven generations back, worked in the business of trading for fur from this outpost. Started out with a log cabin and over the decades his sons and their sons built this manor house. That's why it has a turret and a wall, see. It was a dangerous business."

Mrs Duquette bustled around them collecting the plates. He refilled his whisky glass for what seemed like the hundredth time. Victoria, who loved to learn, surprised herself by blurting out a question.

"What happened next?"

His face fell, and he leaned back into his chair. Looking down at his place setting, he threw back a slug of whisky before continuing.

"By the 1800s, the Europeans had found ways to use less beaver fur, and anyway they were getting hunted out here. Fewer pelts came out of the rivers, and by this point they were worth pennies. The glory days were over, and the Hudson's Bay Company moved on, to timber and oil, and eventually stores, as you probably know. The land itself was more valuable than the animals in it, and the company sold their lot to the country of Canada. As the generations passed, the fur trade all but disappeared, and this manor house went from being the centre of the world to the middle of nowhere."

He seemed genuinely sad now and thumbed the rim of his beaver fur hat. Dyani, who always saw the best in people, almost felt some sympathy.

"Being isolated suits me just fine. I don't like people. But this place won't fix itself, and I'm getting too old to do everything. We need money here. So we're going to have people visit and view the bears. Mrs Duquette suggested we do a trial run with school children, and here you are."

He went to pour some whisky but found the bottle empty. His chair screeched on the floorboards as he abruptly stood up.

"Put the sign in the shed. We'll put it up when the road's clear."

Then he went back to his side of the building.

As Mrs Duquette cleared away the glasses, Jack asked her if there was a phone with which they could check in with their parents. She shook her head sadly.

"There's only one phone in this property and it's in Mr Lagrave's office," she said quietly.

"Can we use it?" he asked.

She laughed under her breath and continued whispering to the children, checking all the time for any footsteps outside the dining room.

"You're joking, aren't you?"

"Why wouldn't he let us? We can pay for the calls," suggested Knievel.

She peered down the hallway to check the Walrus was nowhere in sight, then whispered nervously.

"I've been living here for twelve years and never got to use the phone. When my mother was in hospital with bronchitis in 1968 he refused to let me speak to her. I sent a letter, but it got to her too late. I never got to say goodbye. I've only ever seen the inside of that office once or twice when he left the door open, let alone been inside to use the phone. You can ask him, but I wouldn't. I mean I really, really wouldn't."

The children carried the bear sign outside to the shed and stood it neatly at one side, covering it in a cloth and closing the door. They came in, brushed their teeth in the communal bathroom and put on their pyjamas. The house was cold in the evenings, no matter how many logs they put onto the fire that each of them had in their rooms.

Lance went to sleep thinking about his mum and how warm her voice would sound right now. How he wished he was in his own bed, even if that meant being in the same house as his brothers and father.

Chapter 8

Telephone

The next day the group was given tasks upon awakening, and Lance was paired with Victoria to dust the manor house.

The ceilings of the property were high, and the walls had wooden panelling which culminated above head height with a horizontal picture rail. This gathered dust, as did the light fixtures that hung down and the alcoves that had once housed oil lamps before electricity was brought to the manor.

The duo meticulously worked their way around the labyrinthine property, constantly climbing up, dusting, and dismounting the steps. Then they would move them across by an arm's length and repeat the process. Their shoulders ached before breakfast had even been served, but they worked quietly and methodically, taking turns to be the ladder mover or the duster.

Having finished the hallway and its intricate clock and antler chandelier, they moved into the east wing with some trepidation. Mrs Duquette had asked them to do the whole downstairs, but this part of the property felt like entering the lion's den.

A long corridor ran around the front and side of the building, and the first doorway led to a lounge. The walls were painted a dull olive green and had cracks that had clearly been forming for decades. A huge painting hung above a wide fireplace, showing a hunter standing with a rifle. On the opposite wall was the enormous taxidermied head of a moose. Continuing the theme of dominance over the local fauna was a stuffed beaver in a glass case. Tatty antique furniture was dotted through the room, including a faded salmon-coloured sofa with clawfoot legs. Side tables held crystal decanters, which were empty. The only signs of life from recent times were the ash on the fireplace and a pile of fishing magazines next to a velvet upholstered armchair. Lance and Victoria spent half an hour dusting the room and moved on to the library next door.

This was an impressive double-height room with a vaulted ceiling. Dark wooden shelves with intricate carvings ran from floor to ceiling, covering every wall save for the door and the window. A gallery encircled the room at the second storey, with a simple reading chair perched in the corner. Victoria groaned, as she knew the amount of dust gathered on the tops of books would take hours to clean. The floor of the room had a couple of armchairs and a spiral staircase leading up to the gallery. Conveniently for the cleaners, it had a wooden ladder that could be moved around to access the books and dust the shelves.

Mrs Duquette brought them tea at ten o'clock in the morning, and they took the risk of sitting in the armchairs, which looked out over the east side of the grounds. They recognised the shed where Lance had spent the previous day painting.

With an hour to go until lunch, they finished the last corridor on the ground floor and innocently pushed open the panelled wooden door at the end of it.

The final room was dark and dirty, with books and bottles piled on the floor, thick with dust. The wastepaper basket overflowed, and wooden cases with the silhouettes of wine bottles stamped onto the side were stacked as tall as the kids.

A desk faced the window to the back of the property, next to which sat a hollow globe, which was opened to reveal several bottles of whisky and gin. On the desk was a typewriter and a pot with some pens. Lance and Victoria knew this must be Mr Lagrave's mysterious office, and their hearts began to beat harder. They looked around and saw a gun safe, open and empty.

"Look," whispered Victoria excitedly. On top of the gun cabinet she had noticed a pistol alongside a wooden box with tiny glass darts, each the size of a fat pen lid. The gun itself was long and unusual in that its barrel was square and not round. It looked somehow agricultural, dented and paint worn, as if it had been used regularly as a tool rather than a weapon for once-in-a-lifetime self-defence. The duo hastened to leave, but as they backed out of the room, Lance paused.

"Wait," he whispered, tiptoeing back towards the desk, on which he had spotted a black telephone. His eyes were wide with excitement and fear, and he looked back at Victoria, who stood by the door, shaking her head rapidly.

"Let's go!" she hissed urgently.

Before he knew what he was doing, Lance picked up the receiver and heard the dial tone. Barely able to control his shaking, he put a finger into the dial and rotated the ring of numbers to enter his home phone number. He held the earpiece and listened to the tones as the call was connected. It rang, and Victoria darted in and out of the doorway to keep checking for Mr Lagrave. The phone rang over and over.

A bead of sweat ran down from Lance's hairline.

"Hang up! We have to go!" said Victoria, darting in and out in a panic. She left once more, closing the door behind her.

The phone continued to ring, and Lance clung to that handset so hard his fingers went white. Finally his mum answered, and he cried with emotion at hearing her voice.

"Mom!" he said, tears rolling down his cheeks.

"Hey honey, how's your week going? We've been thinking about you and wondering! None of the moms have heard anything; we wondered if the phones were down. Anyway, how are you?"

As soon as there was a pause in the conversation, he heard a floorboard creak behind him. A cold shiver ran through his body. Without turning around, he exhaled to calm himself and said:

"I'm fine, Mom. Everything's good."

"That's great, honey! We heard there was stormy weather up there and we were starting to get worried, but it's so good to hear your voice."

"You too, Mom."

"Hey, you left your paintbox on the ground in the school parking lot! Jack's mom spotted it on her way to the store and brought it in for us."

"Oh, yes," he said. He looked through the window out onto the back of the property grounds and saw movement in the reflection behind him. He knew he had no choice now but to play innocent and hope for the best.

"It's okay, the owner of this place gave me some paints to use."

"Oh, that's wonderful! Have you seen a polar bear?"

"Yes Mom, plenty of bears here. And I painted one yesterday for Mr Lagrave."

The great Walrus walked around the desk and put his finger onto the receiver, ready to hang up.

"I've got to go now, Mom. Just let everyone know we can't easily make calls but we're okay."

The Walrus nodded.

"Bye, Mom," Lance said, tasting a salty tear as it drained into the corner of his mouth.

"Bye, son. See you in four days!"

Mr Lagrave calmly pressed down on the receiver and took the telephone handset from Lance, who quivered with fear. The Walrus brought the handset to his ear and listened to check it had been disconnected.

He suddenly flipped, swinging the plastic handset into the side of the boy's head and knocking him instantly to the floor. He crouched over him and continued to pummel him in the head as Lance screamed and put his hands around his skull to protect himself.

"You want to use my telephone?" he screamed, beating at his victim like a neanderthal with a bone. He stared down at the dazed boy, who was clutching his head and had blood dripping through his knuckles.

"You want to use my telephone?" he screamed again.

Lagrave now stood up suddenly, grabbing the base unit of the telephone and raising it into the air. The curly wire that connected the handset to the base unit hung between his two hands, swinging against his balding head. With his hands high in the air, his eyes followed the cable which was now taut from the telephone to the wall socket. This seemed to enrage him more, and with a violent outburst he yanked it even further from the wall and the cable finally snapped. The Walrus threw the two parts of the telephone down onto the floor and stamped on them violently with his great black boot. Lance cowered on the carpet with his hands over his head as the brute smashed his foot down repeatedly. Over and over again he pulverised the device, and Lance decided this was his only opportunity to escape.

While Lagrave was focused on the destruction, Lance scrambled past the tree trunks of his legs to the door. Fumbling desperately to open the handle, he managed to pull it open and dashed out into the corridor, crawling on all fours. He and Victoria, who had heard the sickening cries from outside the door, ran down the hallway back towards their bedrooms. They heard the door of the office slam and turned to see if he was chasing them, but thankfully he had closed it from the inside.

The two children scrambled along the corridor that led from Lagrave's office to the hallway. Past the stuffed polar bear they ran, up the stairs and into the dorm room. Victoria paused for a moment on the landing to check Lagrave was not following them. Thankfully he had remained in his den.

Lance slumped on the bed, parting his hair with his fingers to feel if his head was bleeding. Dyani was there in an instant and inspected it carefully.

"It's mostly your hands that took the damage, by the looks of things," she said sympathetically.

Within ten minutes, the rest of the children had gathered in the dormitory, taking turns to periodically step out onto the landing and check for the Walrus. They sat on the floor of the dorm room, on the carpet between the beds at the sides of the room. They leaned their backs against the wooden bunks and rested their feet on the bear rug in the middle of the room. Dyani had nicknamed this the Valley of the Bear. They talked quietly because they were convinced Lagrave was listening somehow, through the air vents or maybe just the other side of the wall with a glass.

Knievel and Freddy played a game of crazy eights, with one ear to the conversation. The rest of them were on edge and focused on the increasingly fraught situation they found themselves in. Lance held a cold, wet towel to his face because Victoria said it would help the bruising.

"I'm sorry I couldn't warn you," she said. "He literally walked towards me with the gun barrel pointing at my head and his finger to his lips. I was terrified."

Lance nodded understandingly, knowing there was nothing she could have done. His cheekbones were painfully bruised and his knuckles were grazed where he had protected his head from the attack.

Jack, who sat twisting Lance's Rubik's Cube without much strategy or success, was impressed at his roommate's quick thinking. "I'll bet every bone in your body wanted to scream 'Call the cops!' down that phone. But you did the smart thing there, buddy. He would have killed you before you'd finished the sentence."

"He won't let us phone the outside world. What does that tell us?" Victoria asked. She gave the group just seconds to consider, before answering her own question. "It means he knows there's a truth that *has* to stay inside these walls. And if he won't even let our *words* leave this property, he sure as hell won't let us leave."

This seemed logical. After all, he could have just locked the office door, but instead he went to the trouble of reducing the telephone to dust.

"Okay," Jack agreed. "So what's the secret he has to keep inside the walls?"

"That he has beaten up kids on a school trip?" suggested Dyani.

"Three times now," added Jack.

The group nodded, and silence fell on the room.

"Are we not going to talk about the fact our driver disappeared?" Victoria said. "I mean, at the time it was a bit weird that he didn't say goodbye and went off in terrible weather. Now we know a little more about Lagrave, it's too suspicious."

Lance got up and walked to the door, opening it to double check nobody was outside. He returned to the Valley and sat back down with the others. He spoke quietly and kept glancing back anxiously to check the door remained shut.

"On the first night, I thought it was strange he was taking black bags of something from the black barn, round the back of the house. You can see it right from this window. And the snow there, you could see footprints – maybe dirt, but it looked bloody to me.

The next day they were gone, and anyway there could be a dozen reasons for that — moving a deer carcass or whatnot."

He whispered so quietly that the boys playing cards had to stop and shuffle over to hear.

"The other day when we were playing hide 'n' seek out front, I saw into that barn and I thought I saw a... hand. Might have been a glove, I still don't know, but it looked like a hand to me. Blood on the concrete. I ran, and that's when he floored me with the snow shovel. He knew I'd seen it and told me he'd kill me if I said a word to anyone."

The others were wide-eyed with this new revelation.

Dyani came over and sat with her roommate, putting her arm around his shoulder.

"You should have told us right away," said Knievel angrily. "How could you keep that from us?"

"Sorry," Lance said, looking down at the claws on the black bear rug. "I thought I must have imagined it, and I didn't want to cause a panic. I mean, it could have been a glove or a part of a deer or something. It's only now I've seen how crazy he can get that I think it could be... human."

Victoria seemed to process the idea of a murder almost instantly and went straight on to the logical implications.

"So let's say he did kill Bob…"

The others almost gasped. Victoria shrugged and continued.

"…and Lance has the only shred of proof. I mean, it'd be your word against his until they find the body, but still. He's got to either make sure you're so frightened you'll keep that secret to your grave. Or, just kill you, too."

"Easy, Vic!" said Dyani.

Victoria shrugged. "You're being naive, Dyani. Anyway, it's not just Lance at stake. Look, Lagrave can't let that information out. Especially now, while there's probably evidence all over the barn. That's why he destroyed the phone. Now he's got a few days left to clean up really well and decide whether he can trust us all. Or else, he'll make us disappear."

"Wait, *all*? Why would he kill me? I ain't seen nothin'. He don't know Babyface spilled his guts to us," said Freddy.

The room went quiet and the kids shifted uncomfortably, as the truth sank in that their lives might be in danger.

"But what if all six of us *and* our driver go missing. How's he going to make that look like an accident?"

"He's a psychopath, Jack. I expect he can figure it out," Victoria said bluntly. "Maybe he'd say at the end of the week we returned, and that's the last he saw of us. Lance didn't mention to his mom that Bob returned home already – did you?"

Lance shook his head, and Victoria continued.

"So as far as our parents are concerned, Bob might have decided to stay up here. We leave on Friday as planned, but never return."

"And an entire bright yellow bus – and its passengers – just disappears?" Freddy said.

Victoria shrugged. "I'm just saying he might be planning something."

"I dunno, man," Knievel said. "I don't think he does a whole lotta planning. He ain't like you, Victoria, working out schemes and alibis. He does a whole lotta *drinkin'*, but not too much thinkin'. My old man's the same, although he wouldn't appreciate the comparison."

"You're both probably right," said Jack, diplomatically. "But we don't need to work out whether he's an unpredictable madman or a calculating psychopath. We just need to get the hell away from him."

Everyone agreed finally, and as usual it was Victoria who came up with the plan.

"Tomorrow morning, straight after breakfast, let's just run down that driveway and get in the bus. Clear the snow around it, start her up and drive down to

James Bay Road. He never gets up before 8 AM. We're up at 6 AM shovelling snow. That gives us a clear two hours."

"What about Mrs Duquette?" asked Lance.

"Are you worried she'll see us?" asked Dyani.

Lance mumbled and looked down.

"You wanna bust her out like a knight in shining armour? Jeez Louise," said Freddy. "We ain't telling her about this. She'll just run to papa!"

Lance sighed. He knew Freddy was probably right, but he saw so much of his mum in Mrs Duquette that he felt awful leaving her here.

Shortly after their discussion, she called the group down for lunch. She was horrified to see the injury on Lance's face and fingers. He told her what had happened, and she gasped hardest at the part when he admitted they had walked into Mr Lagrave's office.

She crouched next to Lance and said, "I'm sorry he is this way. I'm proud of you for making that phone call. To hear your mom's voice. That must have been really special." Her eyes began to well up as she reminisced about her own mother's final weeks and how she had not been allowed to speak to her.

Within minutes, she had put on her fake smile and was serving plates of smoked salmon and capers, with bread she had baked that morning. The Walrus rang a bell that indicated he would take his lunch in his turret, where he often spent his days drinking and watching out over his kingdom.

That afternoon the kids played in the grounds, being sure to stay in the west side of the manor where they could not be overlooked by the monster.

Lance could not understand how the others could play so freely, despite knowing that tomorrow they would risk death to escape. He wished he too could shut that fear and paranoia into a box and simply set it aside while he ran around in the deep snow with his new friends. With a heavy heart, he sat on a wood stump used to split firewood and watched them.

Dyani noticed and came over to him.

"What's up? Not in the mood for chase?"

Lance shook his head in frustration. "I can't get him out of my head. The shovel, the guns, the telephone. How can he get away with this? There are six of us and one of him, and yet we're constantly on the run."

"Don't worry. We'll get out of here tomorrow," she said optimistically, squeezing him across his shoulders. "Come play!"

Chapter 9

Escape

Mrs Duquette woke the children up at 5:45 AM, ready to start their chores at six. They were not sure if Lagrave had insisted they continue these daily, or if the dutiful housekeeper thought it safest to simply continue doing so until told otherwise. Anticipating a long, cold journey back home, Dyani wore two pairs of socks and a pair of jeans underneath her dungarees.

The kids all put whatever valuables they had into their pockets, although for most of them this was just a pen or a cheap watch. Lance took the Rubik's Cube his mother had given him. Today was the day they would leave, unbeknownst to the adults in the house.

It was dark when they went outside with their snow shovels, insisting to Mrs Duquette that they would all work together today and complete their chores in this order. They said clearing the snow was best done before breakfast, while they were fresh.

Lance took a final look at the menacing stuffed polar bear and the paintings that decorated the hallway. He hoped he would never have to see this madhouse again as he followed the others down the stone steps for the final time. It was dark outside, but the snowy ground reflected so much of the moonlight that it was easy to see their way. Thankfully it was not snowing, although the frigid air was bitter and felt like it was burning the exposed skin on their faces.

The group methodically worked their way along the driveway with their shovels, clearing a path as the boys had done on previous days. They caught each other's glances now and then, to check whether this was really going to happen. Despite the icy cold wind snapping at their faces, the atmosphere was electric.

At 6:20 AM they had made it to the front gates, and they all looked back at the house. They saw no light coming from the windows and could make out no silhouette in the turret. With the coast clear and freedom within reach, Freddy weaved his snow shovel through the gap between the bars and became the first to make a break for it.

He reached up and gripped the thick metal bars, hauling himself up to a horizontal metal brace, and then up past the O in Fort. He worked quickly but calmly, so that the two halves of the gate would not clang together. Once over the top, he lowered himself down until he was about his own body height above the snow, and then dropped the rest of the way. His legs were buried up to his waist, and on any other day it would have made the others laugh. Today the stress levels of the group were too high for that.

Now over the other side, Freddy surveyed the area for signs of a bear, rearming himself with his shovel, for what good it would do.

The others followed him one after the other, and with barely a whisper they were soon out in the wild. They waded through the thick snow for the few hundred metres to the bus and immediately set to work to clear a path in front of it. It was leaning at an angle where one side the wheels were on the submerged road, and the other on the verge.

The six children sweated in the cold night air, their breath blowing grey clouds of vapour. They dug out the sides and back and then cleared away the snow in a path that led back onto the road. The road itself had snow on it up to their knees though, and Lance wondered what would happen once they got to the end of the short runway they had dug out.

Still, this was no time for pessimism. They were flushed with adrenaline and reassured that still no lights were on in the house, except for the dining room where they knew Mrs Duquette would be working. Even more importantly, there was no sign of a marauding bear.

With the bus itself cleared and the snow around it removed, Jack yanked the door handle. It was frozen shut and required all his force to do so, but finally it sprung open, showering him with snow and making a clunk. The group grimaced, but they knew they were far enough from the house that the noise would not be a problem. They climbed aboard as quietly as they could and watched in excitement as Jack sat in the driver's seat and twisted the key, which had been left in the ignition.

A light on the dashboard flickered and a clicking noise came from the engine, but there was no sound of the starter motor turning over. He tried again and again, turning off the heater and radio to ensure nothing else would be competing for battery current.

"It's dead," he said morosely. "The battery is completely dead. And we ain't gonna jump start this on this road. Not even with all six of us pushing. Not in this snow." He rested his head on the top of the steering wheel.

"Then we have to get back, before they realise what we've done," said Victoria. The others looked aghast at the idea of returning to the manor they had just left.

"I'm not going back there. Never," said Freddy. "I'd rather die out here."

Knievel agreed. "Let's just walk out of here! We've got our legs. How many miles was it to the highway? Ten? Twenty at most. We can walk it in a day."

Freddy was adamant, but he could see the others were unconvinced. "Girls, you worked out yesterday he was going to kill us. Now he's going to know we tried to escape. After all, he'll see the snow cleared around the bus. So what good is it going back? Let's walk. At least we have a chance."

Condensation ran down the inside of the bus windows. It was hours till the sun would rise, but the darkest part of the night was long past and the sky was now more blue than black. There was snow in every direction, as far as the eye could see, and outside the air temperature was just below freezing.

Dyani felt teary, and she sniffed, "We have to go back inside. This is bear country. We don't have any water or food, no way of lighting a fire. I don't even have my knife and flint. We walk out into that wilderness, we're as good as dead. If we go back inside, he might beat us. But I don't know if he's going to kill us. Not today, anyway. Then we can make a new plan."

"Yep," said Victoria. "I'd rather take my chances with that old fool than the world's largest polar bear. There are wolves and all sorts out here too."

"We have to stay together," said Jack. "I'll go either way, but we ain't splitting up. We can't have two girls going into a house with a madman, and others wandering out into the wilderness."

They all nodded, even Knievel and Freddy. Splitting up seemed like the worst option of all, as staying together was always the first rule of survival in books they had read.

"That's two votes apiece. What about you, Lance?"

The whole bus was now focused on Lance, who was sitting in the black bench towards the front of the bus, which he had originally chosen in Matagami. He looked out of the windscreen at the dark manor house, in what felt like a deja-vu. Except this time, he had a choice — stay, or go. His first instinct was to run and never look back. But something had changed.

"I always run. From my brothers, my dad... you, Freddy. My mom, she runs from my dad too. We literally hide in the woodshed together most afternoons, making up stories and stuff to kill the time until their tempers have simmered down and we can go cook their dinner. But it isn't right. He is there making us all scared for our lives. And what, because he's big? Big man, with his big gun. I hate him more than anybody I've ever hated. I want to get out of here. I really do." He swallowed, his thoughts crystallising in his head as he spoke. "But I'm not running anymore. I'd rather he killed me here and now and be done with it than always be running. I'm going back inside."

The young boy, the smallest of them all, stood up and opened the door of the bus, climbing down the steps. Dyani followed, and Victoria. Freddy looked at Jack, who shrugged apologetically and followed Lance, picking up his snow shovels and trudging back towards the gates.

Even Knievel begrudgingly followed them, shaking his head and spitting into the snow with irritation. Freddy rested his head on the metal bar on the back of his seat, looking at the ceiling of the bus. Despite his claims he'd rather die alone outside, he reluctantly stormed out of the bus and closed the door.

"Wait up," he said quietly to the others.

They hurled their shovels over the wall like javelins, then carefully climbed back over. The house was still dark, and with great humiliation and defeat, they resumed their shovelling of the driveway. At 8 AM Mrs Duquette banged on a metal pot to call them in for breakfast.

Chapter 10

Red Paint

After lunch, the group played outside as they had done for the previous few days. This time they ventured around the back of Fort Lagrave, where they could hide among a clutch of trees inside the grounds. They were well out of earshot of the house, and they checked often to ensure Lagrave was not in the turret. He had been keeping a low profile since he'd attacked Lance with the telephone the previous morning.

"Looks like we got away with it," said Victoria to the others.

"I saw him at lunchtime, and he saw me from the hallway. He didn't say anything," said Dyani, confirming her hunch. "So either he hasn't noticed that we dug the bus out, or he doesn't care."

The group had been at Fort Lagrave for four nights. On Saturday they had arrived. On Sunday Lance had seen into the barn and been hit with the shovel. On Monday, Lagrave had made them start cleaning the house every morning, and Lance had painted the sign. Tuesday was the terrible affair with the telephone. Now it was Wednesday, and their pre-dawn escape attempt had failed miserably. Despite the general sense of impending doom and the disaster of not being able to start the bus, the kids made the best of their afternoon. They played in the gardens and tried to keep out of the way of the Walrus.

The children split into two teams, with Victoria leading one and Freddy the other. They played snowball war, which was slightly more strategic than a normal snowball fight in that you could only get hit once before you were struck out. Victoria's team – with Dyani and Lance – hid behind the trunks of the pine trees. The remaining boys stalked them from around the walls of the house and behind the sheds and barns.

Lance watched Knievel creep up and tried to warn his teammate, but Dyani couldn't hear him and a snowball came crashing down on her back as she crouched.

"Dyani is OUT," shouted Knievel triumphantly. She remained crouched over, wriggling briefly to make the snow tumble from her back.

Lance – suicidally – walked over and crouched beside her. As predicted, he was killed instantly by a snowball at the hands of Jack, who came to join them.

"What's up, Dyani?" Lance asked.

She was crouched over a path that ran from the front of the house, up through the trees she was under, and towards the wall at the rear of the property. The path was marked by muddy footprints and tyre tracks from a wheelbarrow, and it was peppered with twigs and mud. Among the debris on the dense snow was a tiny fragment of white.

"That's a bone," she said, picking it up. It was about the size of a pencil, snapped in two, and she carefully inspected the end that revealed the hollow interior.

Jack shrugged. All the meat they had been consuming in this remote house had been hunted by Mr Lagrave, and it was no surprise that there would be animal residue around the grounds.

"You see how the outside of this bone is thin, compared to the hole in the middle?" she said, lifting it between the tips of her fingers.

"I think so. But I haven't ever seen a bone snapped in half before, so I can't compare," Lance admitted.

"Animals have thicker walls in their bones, and not much cavity in the centre. I've skinned a lot of deer and

I know this isn't one. It's also fresh – you see how white that bone is?"

"So what is it?" Jack asked.

"Judging by the curve and size, I think this is a human rib."

Jack and Lance froze for a second, feeling a wave of cold go over them that made the hairs on the back of their heads stand up. Freddy, Knievel and Victoria had joined them now, and they huddled around the bone. Dyani explained again to the newcomers why she thought it was a human bone.

"You know this from your tipi culture? Have you, like, killed people?" Freddy asked with genuine curiosity.

"No!" She punched him in the shoulder and Freddy toppled over into the snow. "I just watch cop shows. Believe it or not, we do have a television. In our HOUSE."

She slipped the bone into her pocket, and the children fanned out along the pathway that snaked up through the snow towards the wall. They stooped over the dirty trench of snow in the shadow of the pine trees, searching for more fragments of bone.

Victoria followed the path all the way to the end, where she noticed a stack of wooden pallets had been placed. She was desperate to see what was on the other side of the wall, but she hesitated to climb them in case

Lagrave was watching. She returned to the others and suggested they resume playing snowballs, because she was too paranoid about him looking out of the window of the library or office and seeing them acting suspiciously. They had found no more evidence of human – or animal – remains and agreed that they should not push their luck.

The kids resumed playing at the sides of the property, which seemed to be most protected from the gaze of the tower. As the afternoon drew on, they tired and returned indoors to sit in the Valley of the Bear and await dinner.

"So, you think it's Bob's rib bone?" Knievel asked Dyani.

"Well, yeah!" Victoria interrupted.

"How sure are you, though?" he replied. Victoria pounced again to answer.

"Bob mysteriously disappears. Lance sees a human hand. Dyani finds his rib. How sure do you need to be, Kevin? You hoping to find a death certificate?"

He raised his eyebrows as if to say, 'okay, okay,' and went back to playing poker with Freddy.

"So we just sit here waiting for this bomb to blow us all into the sky? He's too damn unpredictable. He makes no sense at all."

Lance narrowed his eyes slightly, which Freddy spotted.

"What you looking like that for, sparrow-boy? You think he's perfectly normal, don't cha? Cos you're a weirdo too!"

The others all looked now at Lance, who felt uncomfortable being the centre of attention in the quiet room. He breathed slowly and deeply, then tried to overcome his nerves and explain his thoughts.

"I don't think he's normal. I don't think he's completely unpredictable, either. My mom says…"

"Oh jeez, what does your mommy say about axe murderers? This I *have* to hea…"

"Shut up, Freddy, and let him talk," said Jack.

The room fell silent again and Lance continued.

"You say he's an unpredictable bomb and there's nothing we can do except hide. But the thing is, bombs aren't unpredictable, are they? They're full of explosives and when you light a fuse, they blow up. It's quite predictable."

That made sense to the group, although some of them failed to connect it back to the situation at hand.

"So we have to figure out his fuse," said Victoria, nodding. She liked to think of herself as the genius of the group, and she was impressed – even jealous – that Lance's train of thought had steamed ahead.

"Well, I can answer that one," said Knievel. "Gin. Rum. Wine. That's his fuse. Case closed."

"Well, he's right ain't he? Sherlock Holmes, got any other insights from yo' mama?" said Freddy, bitingly. "Maybe she's on the phone right now. Oh, no, wait a minute…"

"Freddy, shut up for once! He actually has something useful to say, so let him speak. Not everyone who drinks hits kids with shovels," Jack said. After a short silence in which Lance gathered up the thoughts that had filled his sleepless nights, he continued his analysis.

"To be *that* full of hate, you must hate yourself. Yes, my mom told me that, and I believe it. Lagrave…"

Lance instinctively lowered his voice at the mention of his name, checking the door was shut out of paranoia, and continued.

"He's like a balloon, full to bursting with hatred and self-loathing. The tiles on the roof tumble down onto that balloon. The drips from the ceiling he's too broke to fix. That heavy gaze of his oh-so-successful ancestors with their medals. The weight of a whole lifetime of failure. It's all weighing down on him, pushing and pushing on that balloon. And he drinks to run from it, but it's all there inside of him. And that balloon only has a thin skin."

The room fell quiet as the group absorbed the picture. Freddy clapped his hands together slowly.

"So… can I speak now?" Freddy asked Jack, sarcastically. "How does that help, scrawny-boy? Like, at all. What, you gonna write a poem called 'The Balloon That Killed'? Make your fortune? Oh no, you ain't, because we're gon' die in here 'fore you have a chance."

Knievel smirked at the mention of 'The Balloon That Killed', and the moment moved on. It was coming towards dinner time and Victoria headed across the landing to the shower, and Freddy and Knievel returned to their room to get changed.

"I'd buy your poem," Dyani whispered with a sweet smile.

"Thanks, Dyani," he laughed.

They were nervous as they dressed for dinner. Mrs Duquette had washed and ironed their shirts, and the kids assumed she too must be treading on eggshells.

The children sat nervously around the dining table when the Walrus entered the room, a half-full bottle of whisky dangling from his hand. He cavorted in, clearly drunk, twirling around theatrically and raising the bottle towards the painting of one of his ancestors standing over the body of a polar bear.

"Trust you had a good day," he grunted. The kids nodded.

He pulled out his dark wooden chair and fell heavily into it.

"Trust," he grunted inaudibly, pouring himself a glass of red wine and swilling it around, as if he were now a connoisseur and not a desperate alcoholic.

"Trust is important. In the army, if you haven't got trust, you're as good as lost," he mumbled, looking round at the children's faces individually.

"Trust and respect is what nations are built on," he continued, pouring himself a glass of whisky.

They looked down at their plates, eager to avoid eye contact with the beast.

"I see you dug the bus out."

Silence hung over the table like a guillotine waiting to drop.

"Are you going to tell me why?" he said, sitting back in his chair and raising his glass to his lips. The children looked at each other, not knowing what to say. Jack took the lead.

"Lance wanted to see if his box of paints was in there," he said, his eyes not leaving his plate.

"Is that right? You again," he said menacingly, leaning forward towards Lance.

Lance was sitting next to Lagrave and couldn't help but smell his foul breath. The young boy looked down at his place setting, with his fingers gripping the wooden table to the sides of his cutlery. He spoke with a shake in his unbroken voice.

"I thought you might want me to do more painting, so we were looking for my paints. Thought we'd dig it out."

Lance's fingers made a tiny, nervous adjustment to his fork.

Suddenly the Walrus snatched the fork and stabbed it down into Lance's left hand, piercing the skin. The boy screamed in pain and yanked it away, clutching his left hand with his right.

The Walrus leaned in and shouted, "You wanted some more colours. There's your red!" He cracked an evil grin. "Don't lie to me, boy. That goes for all of you."

The others froze, desperate to get out of there and comfort Lance, but paralysed with fear. Lance screeched back his chair and wrapped a napkin around his hand, on which a red spot of blood appeared immediately. He ran out of the dining room and up the stairs, quickly followed by Mrs Duquette, who burst through the kitchen doors on hearing the scream.

"For God's sake!" said the Walrus angrily as he watched his housekeeper disappear. After a few minutes passed in a deafening silence, he stood up and turned around to go into the kitchen, knocking his chair over in the process. He huffed across the room and kicked the swinging kitchen doors open angrily.

The kids heard him swear in the kitchen as he burned his fingers opening the oven door. He removed a roasting dish containing a long haunch of venison with a thigh bone so thick and long it had to be put into the stove diagonally. He carried the dish into the dining room with a towel and Dyani hastily cleared an area on the table for it. Shaking his head with rage at having to serve his own dinner, he banged the metal pan onto the tablecloth. He yanked at the meat with his fork and filled his own plate. The children watched on, not daring to get involved.

Mrs Duquette came running down the stairs and through the dining room. "He needs stitches," she said matter-of-factly.

"And it's now twenty after eight and I haven't got my dinner!" he shouted back.

"He needs stitches, in his hand," she said defiantly. Her face was red, and the children were terrified at the tension rising.

"So you keep saying!" he shouted at her. "And *I* need my jelly!"

Mrs Duquette paused for a moment, then opened the door that led from the dining room up to her living quarters. When she returned with a needle and thread, the Walrus stood up in a furious rage and picked up the roasting dish of venison, hurling it across the room at her.

"Aaagh!" she screamed as the pan clattered against the wall, sending a splash of hot fat onto her bare leg. The meat rolled across the wooden floor and its gravy poured out of the upturned pan into the cracks in the boards. Still, she ran up to Lance's room in defiance of her master.

The Walrus stood up and skulked out of the room, shouting, "What are you looking at?" to Jack as he passed. He continued down the corridor to the east wing and holed up in his library, where he dined on whisky for main course and rum for dessert.

Up in the boys' bathroom, Mrs Duquette had cleaned up the wound with surgical spirits and it had finally stopped bleeding. It was a narrow but deep cut and needed a stitch. In a remote region like this, several hours from the nearest hospital, it was quite common to treat even severe injuries at home.

She told Lance to be brave and bite down on a towel if the pain was too much. She inserted the needle and his eyes watered with the agony that shot through his hand and up his arm. After a minute or two – which felt like forever to Lance – she was done, and four neat stitches held the wound closed. She sat with him on a wooden bench in the shower room and helped him hold his hand aloft, as he was feeling faint. When the throbbing subsided and his head became clearer, he thanked her.

"When you went to the office, what was in there?" she asked quietly, still holding up his bandaged hand.

"It had piles of papers and mail on the floor. Letters and stuff. There was the telephone, obviously. But he smashed it to pieces, so that can never work again. Lots of crates of wine, or whisky or something in bottles. Oh, and speaking of bottles, there was a weird little gun with tiny syringes. I described it to Jack, who lives on a farm. He said it sounded like a tranquiliser gun."

"Describe the room again," she asked, seemingly fascinated by the last secret in a building she knew only too well.

Lance mapped it out for her, recalling every item he could, from pots of pens to books on shelves. She thanked him and told him again how brave he was, and that she wished she could have had a son just like him.

Chapter 11

Mrs Duquette

Lance noticed that Mrs Duquette was nervous at breakfast. She mopped the sweat from her brow even though the room was fairly cold. Later he heard a plate smash in the kitchen. Everyone was grateful that Mr Lagrave had not joined them that morning.

After breakfast, the children worked outside again. It had snowed again in the night, and where the wind had blown the snow in, the gates were buried up to waist high.

Up on the turret, the Walrus sat on a wooden barrel. It was uncomfortable to sit for hours without being able to recline, but he had run out of chairs in the house to bring up. One by one they had been brought up to the turret and eventually rotted by the relentless rain and snow. Now he had to resort to sitting on wine barrels and beer kegs. Day after day of his miserable life he had sat up in the turret, surveying his kingdom and occasionally taking a shot at a distant moose or white-tailed deer.

He surveyed the landscape with his binoculars, watching the Great White Bear pad across a rocky escarpment at the edge of the lake. The black granite rocks under his feet had jagged, slanting layers like a chain of dominos that had been toppled. The bear was a thing of beauty to Lagrave, and one of the only things that could make him smile. A magnificent lumbering mass, unafraid of anything and anyone. As close as he had to a child.

"Come on, boy. Lunchtime," he muttered, panning his binoculars across to just outside the walls of his estate, as if his thoughts alone could lure the bear across the tundra. There he could see that the meat he had slung over the wall earlier that day was still there. A human leg, complete with a brown leather boot.

Lagrave's rifle was resting precariously against the grey stone crenelations, and it fell to the floor when the turret door swung open. Amid the clatter, he turned in surprise to see Mrs Duquette, shaking, with both hands on a pistol.

Her arms were straight, making a sharp, strong triangle pointing right at Lagrave's chest. The Walrus was motionless on his seat as he drank in the unfamiliar situation of Mrs Duquette asserting her power. The still air was frozen and her short, panicked breath made white clouds of vapour.

He was still at first, and then his leathery, wrinkled face cracked into a confused look. He rocked forward, ready to heave himself to standing.

"Sit down!" she ordered.

"Or what?" he said, continuing to stand up. He towered over her from just an arm's length away.

The children in the garden had heard their voices and now assembled in front of the house, staring up at Mrs Duquette pointing the gun at her captor's chest. She was shaking, with her right finger on the trigger of the pistol.

"Twelve years you've kept me here. Prisoner in this *hole*," she said, trembling, with tears running down her face.

"Kept you here? You could have left any day you wanted. Remember you had nothing when you came here, Duquette. NOTHING."

"And what have I got now?" she screamed. "Still got nothing. Waited on you hand and foot for the best years of my life and got nothing. Watched you chop people up and hit kids and sat by and done nothing. Not anymore."

"Put the gun down," he grunted, putting his hands in the air to calm her. "Things are changing now. We've got the bear now. We'll have money."

His promises came too late for Mrs Duquette. She gritted her teeth and squeezed the trigger, blasting a dart from the gun which punctured into his chest, making him stagger backwards. The metal syringe had plunged into his ribs and the chemicals inside it were bursting into his bloodstream. He gasped for breath and grabbed at his chest, too dazed to coordinate his hands and remove the dart.

He stayed on his feet though, to her surprise. She backed up to the doorway, waiting for the drugs to kick in and tranquilise him. She scooped his rifle away behind her with her white shoe. The children in the garden felt a wave of dread coming over them at seeing that Lagrave had not hit the deck.

Lagrave was still on his feet, but barely. His face was scarlet and he choked for breath, as if he'd just emerged from a near drowning. Clearly still in shock from the gunshot, he yanked a glove off and pulled the dart from his chest. He held it between his fingers and brought it up in front of his eyes, seeing that it was empty.

He dropped it to the ground, and it smashed. Slowly and savagely, his focus shifted to the quivering Mrs

Duquette, who was backing up now towards the door frame to the top of the spiral stairs.

"What do you think it is, woman? Poison? Tranquilisers? It's steroids, you fool! How else do you think I managed to create the world's largest bear? But you. After all I've done. You tried to kill me? ME??"

He stepped towards her, swatting the dart gun from her hands. It clattered onto the stone floor of the turret and she turned to run, but he grabbed her by the hair with one hand and yanked her back towards him.

She screamed, and Lance shouted, "No! Please no!" from the grounds.

With steroids coursing through his veins, he felt a massive surge of power and white-hot aggression. He grabbed her blue dress around her thigh and his other massive hand clamped around the back of her neck. He lifted her up with the strength of a gorilla, high above his head. Her pinny and hair blew in the wind, and she screamed and wriggled desperately.

"No!" the children screamed from down in the grounds. Mr Lagrave hurled her from the turret. Her body flew through the air, arms circling frantically as she swam in slow motion through the grey sky. She fell like a stone, smashing into the tiled roof of the library twenty feet below. Her body ragdolled down the steep roof and caught on the guttering, which flipped her in the air, and finally she plummeted to the pathway beside the building. She landed with a deafening thud on the ground, just fifty metres from the children.

Lance led the charge towards her, but before he even reached her he knew she was dead. Her eyes and mouth hung open, and she was completely still. He touched his fingertips onto her neck to check her pulse, but there was nothing. With tears streaming from his eyes, he gently closed her eyelids.

Mr Lagrave opened the front doors and hobbled down the steps, almost tripping over his own feet. His face was bright red and eyes bloodshot as a dosage of steroids designed for a bear weighing half a ton flowed through his veins.

"She fell," he garbled as he reached the youngsters. "Is she okay?

"Mrs Duquette!" he shouted, slapping her face. "Wake up!"

Lance reached out to protect her face from the man's massive hands. He gripped Lagrave's wrist and said, "She's dead."

Lagrave stood up, looking at her for just a moment, and up at the guttering, which was broken around the library roof.

"Then bury her," he replied coldly, turning his back to them. His eyes twitched madly and he blinked over and over again. He staggered back towards the house, almost hobbling, as if he had forgotten how to walk. He paused halfway up the stairs to the front door.

"Over there, by that wall. Set a fire to soften the earth," he called back, motioning to the side wall. This is not the first time he's buried a body, thought Victoria.

Lance sobbed over the dead body of Mrs Duquette, gripping her hand as its warmth faded. The others grabbed the sheet that rested over the polar bear sign in the shed and laid it over her corpse. It felt like the grown-up thing to do. Even Freddy and Knievel were silenced by the horror of what they had witnessed.

After a few quiet hours of contemplation, shock and grief, the kids set to work on clearing a patch of snow to bury her. They dug down to the earth, which was frozen as hard as concrete.

Dyani began to ferry a wheelbarrow loaded with logs from the woodstore to the east wall, and Victoria built a fire. They lit it and the group spent several hours feeding it and quietly talking under the crackle of the flames.

Until now there had been some ambiguity about whether they really had anything to tell the police. Did Lance see a hand or not? It would have been his word against Lagrave's, and the kids had correctly guessed that the remains of Bob's body would never be found.

He would not be the first person to go missing in this untamed wilderness, even if he was just a matter of metres from a property.

But this had changed. There were six eyewitnesses to Lagrave's savage murder of his housekeeper. He could never claim it was self-defence to hurl a woman from a rooftop, even if she had just shot him in the chest with a dart gun. It would be his word against all six children, and the body would show marks of his hand around her neck and thigh.

This was a secret that could never leave Fort Lagrave, and the children sat around that fire wondering when bullets would come raining down from the turret towards them. If they ran, his instinct would be to shoot. Once he had killed one of them, he would have no choice but to hunt them all down like rabbits.

Their situation felt hopeless, even to the optimistic Dyani.

"All we can do is get through today, and hope that he calms down and starts thinking straight," she said.

Victoria, meanwhile, was growing impatient and wanted blood.

"If anyone sees his gun unattended, grab it. If anyone sees any opportunity at all to smash him over the head with a piece of wood or something, do it.

We'll all pile in. We just wait and play nice, and hope for an opportunity. The only other way out is if someone comes to pick us up. We've only got two days left until they expect us home. Surely they'd send a rescue party if we haven't shown up twenty-four hours after that."

At lunchtime they gingerly went into the house and straight through the dining room to the kitchen. They found the refrigerators neatly organised and well stocked, and larders full of tins and jars. Bread had been baked afresh each day by Mrs Duquette, so there was none of that. They made do with tins of potatoes and some venison that she had rescued the previous night.

The children tidied the kitchen up perfectly, desperate not to enrage the Walrus, and went back to the grounds to dig the grave.

They let the fire die out and cleared the ash from the ground, throwing snow on it by the shovelful to melt into the soil and soften it further. Lance angrily stabbed at the ground and hurled the steaming earth onto the surrounding snow. Dyani suggested he take a break and let the others do it, but the young boy insisted on continuing. It seemed to help him process what was happening, or channel his anger. Probably both.

At 3 PM they carried her body – now frozen solid – and lowered her on the sheet into the hole. With her skeletal arms folded across her chest, she looked more peaceful than they had ever seen her.

Lance and Dyani cried, and Jack said a few words that he thought sounded like what an adult would have said. The group hung their heads and closed their eyes.

"Dear Lord, take this beautiful person and look after her in heaven. Ashes to ashes, dust to dust. Amen."

Lance tossed in the first shovel-load of soil onto her body, and the others followed. By the time they had finished, all that was left to show of Mrs Duquette was a mound of soil and a simple wooden cross, which Freddy of all people had hewn from some firewood and tacked together with nails.

Dyani put her arm around Lance and assured him that her spirit would live on in another realm.

Chapter 12

Sing-song

In the late afternoon, the children were in Knievel and Freddy's bedroom when they heard a din of clanging metal almost outside their door. They jumped up and stepped out onto the landing to see Mr Lagrave down by the stuffed polar bear, with a huge metal pot in one hand and a wooden spoon in the other.

"Dinner is at eight. See that you make it," he shouted up at them.

They nodded, and he let the pot clang on the floor and skulked off down the hallway into the east wing.

"'See that you make it on time to dinner'? Or 'See that you make my dinner'?" asked Knievel.

"What do you think?" Victoria replied sarcastically. "You reckon he's got an apron and is going to rustle us up something nice?"

With two hours to go, they made their way to the kitchen and surveyed the pantry and fridge. There was a cooked ham wrapped in aluminium foil, which seemed the easiest option.

Victoria suggested they cook some baked potatoes with ham, which seemed fine to the boys, but Dyani worried how the Walrus would react to such a basic dinner.

"She normally cooks dolphin potatoes or whatever. Fancy stuff. He might go crazy if we serve up just some ham and potato."

Lance was past caring what Mr Lagrave might do to him next. He had been punched, beaten and stabbed. It felt futile to try to avoid his wrath. He knew he could defrost some chicken and make a fine chasseur. Or fry some moose steaks in garlic with mashed potatoes and gravy. But why should he? This murderous monster had killed the only good person he knew in the most brutal way. So he kept quiet and nodded when the group concluded that dinner would be ham, baked potatoes and his all-important jelly.

Eight o' clock came and the group were ready with dinner. They had laid it out neatly on seven plates and had drawn sticks of spaghetti from a cookbook to decide who had to serve it to the Walrus.

They watched through the porthole in the kitchen door and saw him take his seat just before eight o'clock. As the grandfather clock chimed, Victoria nervously entered the dining room and placed the dish in front of him.

"Ah, dinner is served," said Mr Lagrave, who looked down curiously at the meal. After a few terrifying seconds in which time stood still, he tucked his napkin into the collar of his red shirt and picked up his cutlery.

"Well, sit down, will you," he said.

Victoria returned with the others, and they joined him at the long table. They became nervous when he stood up and went into the kitchen. He returned with a bottle of red wine and a corkscrew. This, it seemed, was the only chore he was capable of doing for himself.

He poured it into his glass, remaining standing. Then he circled the table, filling the remaining six glasses and draining the dregs into his own.

He stood at the head of the table and raised his glass. The children glanced at each other and realised they should follow suit, standing up in a flurry of scraping chairs.

"'Tis a tragic day at Fort Lagrave. A sad and untimely death of a dear friend of mine of twelve years. When she came here, she was all but destitute with not a dollar to her name. I provided for her like a father, for all this time. I gave her great company, warm lodgings and a comfortable life. We drink to Fort Lagrave, and my twelve years of kindness and generosity."

He pushed his glass forward and touched it on the glasses of Freddy and Victoria, who were his closest neighbours this evening. The others chinked their glasses gently together and followed when the Walrus said, "To Fort Lagrave."

They each sipped on the red wine and grimaced at its bitter taste.

Lance seethed with anger and could not stop himself from adding, just at the moment when the Walrus was about to sit down:

"To Mrs Duquette."

The group looked nervously at their host, who thought briefly and conceded, "And to Mrs Duquette."

Again they sipped and grimaced, then sat down to eat their baked potatoes and ham. They were dry, despite the butter, but Mr Lagrave had not complained, to their great relief.

"What will you tell the people of New York City?" said the Walrus as he sliced the foil from a second bottle of red wine with a pocketknife.

The children were confused, and nobody said anything.

"Have you forgotten how to speak? I asked you what you will tell the world about Fort Lagrave."

Jack said cautiously, "We are from Matagami. It's only five hours from here, in Quebec. We will say your manor is home to the world's largest polar bear."

"Yes, it is!" he barked excitedly, banging on the table. "The world's largest polar bear. As big as a Cadillac. They will come from California to see my bear," he reminded them, looking wistfully at the painting of his ancestor standing over a dead polar bear.

"A bear as big as a tank!" he said, pouring more wine. "Children will sing songs of the Great White Bear. *There is a bear as big as a tank,*" he began to sing, with no sense of tune at all. Then his voice trailed off as he murmured, "*the Great White Bear…*" but realised it didn't rhyme.

"*There is a bear as big as a tank,*" he began again, looking into space. Then he looked at the children and got agitated, his face reddening and his hand smashing down on the table, making the plates jump.

"Am I to do everything? Talk, will you, damn children. What will they sing? You can see what needs to be done! *There is a bear as big as a tank.* What comes next?"

The children were perplexed but not completely surprised that this dinner had gone so quickly from a toast to his murdered housekeeper to making up nursery rhymes about a bear.

Victoria, whose brain was as sharp as anyone's, sheepishly broke the silence with a solution.

"There is a bear as big as a whale. Twelve feet from its nose to tail."

BANG. The plates leapt clean off the table again as Mr Lagrave thumped his fist excitedly onto the wood. "Yes, girl! *There is a bear as big as a whale. FOURTEEN feet from nose to tail.* It's good! What's next, girl?" He swigged his wine excitedly.

Lance, haunted by the burial of Mrs Duquette and brooding with anger, wondered what might rhyme with 'It ate our driver.' Bloody saliva? he thought, not daring to smile. He looked down at the black wound on his hand as he picked up his glass of red wine, sipping the warm, bitter liquid. Burying a body at lunchtime and drinking red wine with her murderer at dinner. How long, he wondered, before we all go mad here?

The drip-drip-drip of water into the bucket in the corner was a reminder that the Lagrave timebomb might detonate any second. Dyani rescued Victoria by finishing the impromptu song. She suggested, sheepishly:

"He eats all night and eats all day, the sparkling jewel of Hudson Bay?"

Mr Lagrave concentrated hard to recall the poem. *"There is a bear as big as a whale, fourteen feet from nose to tail. He eats all night and eats all day, the sparkling jewel of Hudson Bay."*

He stood, eyes wide with excitement, wrestling off his shirt and putting it on the back of his chair. He was left wearing a white vest, the fabric brown-stained and tatty. "Children will sing it from Kentucky to Nova Scotia. *There is a bear as big as a whale...*" he chanted, banging his hands on the table with a furious energy. Realising they were expected to join in, the kids began to say it too, half singing and half speaking. Over and over he sang the song, walking around the room and putting his hands on their shoulders, gripping around their tiny necks and shaking them as the pace quickened. Soon they were practically screaming it, racing through the song and starting immediately on the next loop.

Then he stopped and the song trailed off. He took the last of his bottle of red wine towards the east wing, leaving the children to clean up. The room fell silent and the kids all looked to ensure he was not coming back.

"*Sparkling jewel.* That was quite special, Pocahontas," Freddy joked when the coast was clear.

"Well, I didn't hear you come up with anything better," Dyani retorted, a little embarrassed.

"Eats all night and eats all day. Hey Knievel, it's the Very Hungry Caterpillar!" Freddy said.

The girls cleared the plates and escaped his torment in the kitchen, where Jack and Lance washed up. They dared not speak as they did so, in case Lagrave was listening through a wall or about to burst in through the doors.

Jack, Lance and Dyani cleaned the kitchen until the metal surfaces shone, while Victoria took a cloth to wipe the massive dining table.

Mr Lagrave's red plaid shirt hung on the back of the chair, and Freddy, who was wandering around uselessly with Knievel, noticed her looking at it. Knowing the Walrus might return for what appeared to be his only item of clothing, Victoria ignored it and went to the kitchen to find a broom. Curiosity gripped Freddy, though, who wondered if there might be a gun or knife in the pocket.

"Pssst! Knievel, watch the corridor."

His friend darted out and looked across from the opening to the dining room, past the stuffed polar bear and down the east wing corridor. In the distance he could hear the sound of classical music playing in the library and raised his thumb to indicate that the coast was clear.

Freddy plunged his hand into the right pocket and yelped in pain. He whipped it back out, and with it came a glass vial, which fell to the wooden floor and smashed into tiny fragments. The crew in the kitchen heard the yelp and came into the dining room, and they all circled around the chair.

On the floor were tiny pieces of glass and a few drops of liquid. A needle as long as a little finger and a red feather were also among the debris.

"It's a tranquiliser dart," Jack said. "Big one, too. That must be a half inch across – 0.50 calibre. We only use them for cattle."

"Am I going to die?" asked Freddy, examining a tiny pinprick in his right index finger.

"Yes," said Victoria, matter-of-factly. "But not today. It was empty. Look, he has loads and they're all empty."

Victoria carefully lifted out another dart between her fingers and showed it to the group. It looked like a fat glass tube with a needle coming out of one end and a tail feather on the other, to keep it straight in the air.

Victoria lowered the dart back into the pocket and they swept up the fragments of glass from the floor, hoping he would not notice one dart missing. They buried the pieces deep in the sack of rubbish in the kitchen bin.

149

Then they carried up firewood to their bedrooms and lit a fire in each hearth, as Mrs Duquette had done every night until now. The group got ready for bed and gathered in Knievel and Freddy's room, which was slightly further from the east wing.

"I don't get it. Why didn't he collapse when she shot him?" Jack asked. "That's enough tranq to knock out an ox. Within like, ten seconds. Bang. On the floor. He must be a quarter the size of a bull and yet he got stronger. Lifted her clear above his head and..."

"What if it's not tranquilisers in there?" Victoria said. "You can put whatever you like in those syringes, right?"

Lance summarised the quandary. "So he isn't a farmer, and there's no cattle for hundreds of miles. Yet for some reason he's got this gun. He must be shooting wildlife with it, and lots of it if he's carrying around five darts in his pocket. We know that when he got shot with it, it didn't slow him down at all. He was more crazy, if anything. It's like the opposite of a tranquiliser dart."

"Steroids?" Freddy suggested. The others looked at him to continue, not knowing what they were.

"You watch wrestling, right? You think those guys get that big from just lifting weights? Most of them are taking steroids. Weightlifters, bodybuilders, they all take steroids. My uncle in Wisconsin got hooked on it. Testosterone. It's like liquid aggression, and they inject it and get all bulked up."

"You should take some, Lance," said Knievel, squeezing the boy's skinny bicep.

"That would explain why he went so crazy yesterday with Mrs Duquette. But why a gun, if he's injecting himself with steroids?" asked Victoria.

"The Great White Bear," said Lance.

She cocked her head to one side, waiting for more. Lance continued.

"Don't you see? He's shooting it with steroids to make it bigger and bigger."

"Oh, yes!" Victoria said. "That makes sense now. And he's luring it in with meat and bones. That's why there's a trail of bones and blood leading up to the wall at the back. He is literally sitting up on that turret like a sniper, pumping that bear up to make sure it's the world's biggest."

"Sparkling jewel of Hudson Bay, don't ya know," added Freddy. Dyani rolled her eyes.

After the revelation had sunk in, Jack chimed in. "Can you imagine how psychotic that bear is? It's now been trained to come towards human encampments and eat human flesh. When it should be out eating seals, it's eating people. We've seen what that stuff can do. It makes you want to kill, and he's been pumping a bear full of it. Yeesh."

"I bet that's what happened to Bob, the driver," said Lance. "He got out of the bus and got mauled to death before he'd made it ten steps. That's why Lagrave asked why we were sitting out there. Bob never even made it to the gates. So then Lagrave went back out that night and found his remains, and stored them in the barn until he'd all been fed to the bear."

"Why, though?" asked Dyani. "Why not call the sheriff right there and say a bear killed a man? Right now he's gonna be a suspect in a murder. He could have told the truth."

"Because the first thing they'd do is shoot that damn bear, stupid," said Knievel. "Once a bear kills, it has to be shot. He ain't lettin' that bear get shot. It's his pride and joy. The only thing he thinks can save this place."

"Now I'm glad we didn't try to walk out of here after all. That thing is like a shark circling our boat," said Jack.

The six schoolmates sat around for a while longer, trying to play cards but unable to concentrate. They eventually went to bed, and as Lance closed the curtains he peered out of the window towards the cross that marked Mrs Duquette's grave. Night had fallen and he could barely make it out.

Dyani put her arm around his shoulder and said, "It's going to be okay." Lance seriously doubted that was true. Inside was a schizophrenic maniac. Outside was a man-eating giant polar bear. Meanwhile, his mum had probably told all the other parents that the kids were having a great time and not to worry about them.

Chapter 13

More Eggs, Woman!

The six kids were downstairs at 7:45 AM with their hair brushed, nervously eating scrambled eggs on toast and wondering which direction the tornado would enter the room from.

As it happened, Mr Lagrave swept into the room more like a summer breeze than a hurricane. He saluted the painting on the wall as he walked across to his throne, turning 360 degrees to do so and very nearly tripping over his own legs. He wore a green tweed military jacket with a fancy collar and brass-buttoned pockets on the front. Over the top he wore a leather strap that ran from his left shoulder to his right hip, at which point there hung a pistol holster. Except instead of a gun, it had a metal flask jammed into it. His lapels were damp with a dark stain, which the children assumed – depending on whom you'd have asked – was red wine, blood from a polar bear, or the last evidence of Bob.

He picked up some toast from a rack in the middle of the table and buttered it.

"MORE EGGS, WOMAN!" he screamed threateningly at the kitchen. The children glanced at each other without looking up, eager to avoid him noticing. They could now tell he was drunk, which was unusual for breakfast when he was normally hungover. He looked like he had been up all night playing dress-up and drowning his problems in a bottle.

He withdrew the metal flask from his holster and poured a drop of a brown liquid into his glass. He then muttered, "A leader leads from the front" under his breath. He stood up and circled the table, reaching between their heads to pour a little whisky into each of their glasses. None dared refuse, and Knievel even went to the trouble of downing his glass of milk to make room for it.

Lance shuddered. First drinking, next they'd be singing the polar bear song.

The Walrus returned to his end of the table and raised his glass, saying proudly:

"To Fort Lagrave, home of the world's largest polar bear. The jewel of Hudson Bay."

The children repeated his toast and brought the whisky to their lips. Freddy and Jack seemed somewhat comfortable with whisky, having drunk with their dads on hunting trips. They slung the liquid back and wiped their lips on their sleeves. Knievel, who rarely looked before he leapt, threw his back too, and Dyani and Victoria reluctantly joined them, seeing no way out. Lance looked down at the brown liquid and held his breath as he poured it into his mouth. His eyes watered and he was a little bit sick in his mouth, causing his throat to burn for an hour afterwards with a foul taste of whisky and bile.

The Walrus poured himself another and slammed it back, then leaned forward and stared down the table. It was 8:15 AM and he was flushed in the face and wild-eyed, as he had been the previous night.

"We need to bring in the bus," he said intensely. Lance gulped, wondering why the Walrus needed to have their only link to the outside world. That bus was literally their ticket out of there, and he wondered if it was next in line to disappear like snowflakes onto warm earth, just as Bob and Mrs Duquette had done.

"You already got the job started, didn't you? Well, you have to open the gates and push her in."

The children, still reeling from the shot of whisky, felt the sickness turn to dread. Outside they knew the bloodthirsty Great White Bear was looming, waiting to scavenge its next meal. They knew it could run faster than a human, and it was big enough that it must be hungry constantly.

"You get out there after breakfast and push her in. Right up and into the barn over on the west side." He waved his hands and pointed one way, then changed his mind and pointed the opposite way.

"Any questions?"

Lance had several burning questions, starting with 'Are you planning to murder us today?', but asked none. Victoria, whose curiosity was powerful enough to overcome her fear of the Walrus, spoke up. She raised her hand, and Mr Lagrave nodded.

"How will we avoid being attacked by a bear while we push the bus?"

He smiled and nodded. "Excellent question, soldier. I'll be watching over you all as you do it, from the turret. I've shot plenty of animals from up there, and you can rest assured that if a beast comes near, he better be able to outrun a bullet."

Excited now, he stood and did another lap of the table, pouring a second round of whisky for the kids – bigger than the last. He sat back in his chair and grinned, banging his palms scarily on the table. The youngsters jumped, and several of them noticed that he had a red inflamed bump on his wrist with a red dot in the centre of it. This was the strangest mood they had ever seen him in, and Lance wondered if he had got a taste for the steroids and was now recreationally injecting himself with them. He did seem unusually aggressive, with his chanting and table banging.

The Walrus continued to bang his hands down over and over again around his place setting, to form a beat.

"We're going to move the bus. We're going to move the bus," he chanted, staring at each of them in turn with his bulging, bloodshot eyes.

Freddy was the first to slam his palms against the table, clattering his silverware and plates. Others joined until all seven of them beat out the rhythm on the dining table, creating a din that echoed in the high-ceilinged room.

Louder and louder the moustachioed leader repeated the chant, "We're going to move the bus! We're going to move the bus!" until all the kids were singing along with him, mostly just frightened of not joining in, but at least partially infected by the madness of Fort Lagrave.

Then as suddenly as he had started, he stopped. Silence fell across the dining room and he picked up his glass, waiting for the kids to follow suit.

"We're going to move the bus," he said one last time, before slinging half a glass of whisky down his throat.

The children followed his lead and grimaced, staring down at the remnants of their scrambled eggs through teary eyes.

The Walrus screeched his chair back and said simply:

"Get the gate key from the hook and rendezvous outside in fifteen minutes. The key to the snowmobile is in the ignition, in front of the black barn. I'll be on the turret keeping you alive, troops. We're going to move the bus! We're going to move the bus!"

He continued to chant like a child as he disappeared out of the dining room towards the east wing.

The children looked at each other in horror and set off upstairs to get dressed.

"What are you going to wear for this?" Dyani asked Jack, who seemed to be holding it together as well as any of them.

"Hmm. Nothing too bulky. No sense making it difficult for them to stuff me into my coffin," he replied. The rest of them shuddered. Even Freddy was unable to raise a cackle this morning.

The group assembled quickly by the front door, retrieving the jackets and boots they had placed there the previous day.

"Do we have a plan?" Victoria asked. The others looked at her and shrugged, slightly embarrassed.

"I'll drive the snowmobile. I've got one on the farm," said Jack. The rest of them nodded, even though all of them had a snowmobile at home too. For several months per year it was the only way of getting around Matagami.

"I'll take the key," volunteered Dyani, always eager to step up.

"Okay, so let's get the snowmobile," suggested Victoria. "Then we all jump in the trailer, and Jack drives us to the bus. Once we're out there, we have to be quick, obviously. We'll have to dig the path from the bus to the gates, right down to where the ground is frozen solid. Otherwise it won't roll across snow. We'll try just pushing it, with Dyani steering – you're the lightest – and Jack pulling with the sled."

Everyone nodded.

"One of us should stay and look out for bears. Especially the big mutant one. In case *he* doesn't. I'll stand on the bus and keep watch while you dig, until it's time to push."

The group accepted their fate. Lagrave would have been pleased to see their military level of planning, if he hadn't skulked off to find an unopened bottle of rum.

The front door was opened by Knievel and the icy wind blasted into the hallway, showering them with snow before they'd even left the building. They funnelled out into the biting sub-Arctic wind, with Lance near the back. He grabbed the huge metal saucepan and wooden spoon that had been abandoned the previous night by the Walrus when he told them to make dinner.

"That looks helpful," Freddy shouted sarcastically when he saw the pot. The wind was too loud to respond, and the team trudged through knee-deep snow towards the shed. Those at the back benefited from the channel that was created by Jack up front. They made it to the shed and searched it.

Jack picked up a heavy coil of rope and slung it over his shoulder. The others grabbed as many shovels as they could find, and the group left its safety and headed once more into the white abyss.

The children trudged towards the snowmobile and climbed into the trailer, leaving Jack and Dyani on the seat.

Despite a powerful 800 cc engine, the snowmobile could not go much faster than running pace because of the weight of the trailer. Still, within a minute or so they were at the front gate.

Dyani dismounted and removed her mitten to retrieve the massive iron key from her pocket. She tried to insert it into the lock, but it was frozen solid. She banged it with her fist, but it was no use. Ice filled the pencil-sized hole, and no amount of forcing in the key would break it.

Freddy shook his head and jumped off the trailer. He motioned for Dyani to go back to her seat behind Jack. Then, to the shock of everyone on the snowmobile, he undid the flies of his trousers and peed on the lock. The girls put their mittens to their faces to cover their eyes in mock disgust. The steaming liquid melted the snow instantly.

Dyani tossed him the key and Freddy opened the lock triumphantly. He pushed against the gates, and they opened with the creak of metal against metal. As soon as they were both open enough for the trailer to get through, he returned to the trailer.

"My ol' man says, 'If it's stupid and it works, it ain't stupid,'" he said.

"He'd be proud of ya. Finally!" Knievel joked.

Lance looked up at the turret and saw, with some relief, the silhouette of the Walrus against the slate-grey sky. It was the only time he had ever been grateful to see him. The children clung onto the metal sides of the trailer as Jack pulled away into the danger zone. As they left the safety of the wall, the entire group looked around anxiously for any signs of the bear.

At the bus, they jumped off the snowmobile and began to dig frantically. Luckily they had cleared much of the snow a couple of days ago in their pre-dawn escape mission.

Victoria put her foot on the chrome bumper and then climbed up, stepping over the bonnet and up onto the roof. She carried the saucepan and spoon so she could make a racket if necessary, since the wind was howling and the others might not hear her shouts.

Looking north towards the house, her view was the stone wall of the estate. Her only worry there was if an animal stalked along using the wall for cover. Looking south down the road to the property, the view was relatively clear and she could see a long way. East and west of the road were pine trees dotted across snowfields, which would provide excellent cover for a marauding bear. It was there that she focused her attention, turning every five or ten seconds to peer out from all angles.

Jack tied the long rope from the snowmobile to the tow hitch he found under the front of the bus. He figured the pull from the machine would undoubtedly help yank the school bus from its resting place. The rest of the team dug furiously, working their way along the road from the front tyres of the bus to the gates.

They had been outside for just a few minutes when they heard Victoria bang on the saucepan. "BEAR!" she shouted, to their horror. "Coming from the east, maybe 500 yards."

"Let's go!" shouted Jack, and the others immediately dropped their shovels and jumped onto the snowmobile.

Padding towards them from the clutch of pine trees near the road was the Great White Bear. It was truly enormous, with cold black eyes just tiny dots on a sea of dirty fur. Seeing it for the first time from the front, they realised how wide it was. It was shaped like a massive white barrel on legs as thick as trunks. It padded towards the kids, and just in the few seconds it had taken for Victoria to jump down from the roof and board the sled, it was now only a twenty-second dash away from them.

"We're tied up!" shouted Jack. "Cut the rope!" he screamed as the bear lolloped towards them, grunting and growling.

Knievel bravely jumped off the back of the trailer and darted a few metres to grab a shovel. He stood back on the metal surface and with both hands on the wooden shovel handle, he cleaved down at the rope.

The bear sized up its prey from just a stone's throw away. Its snarls shot plumes of vapour from its nose, like an ice dragon.

The curved metal of the shovel glanced off the rope, and again Knievel raised it up and smashed it down vertically on the rope. This time it frayed, and Jack revved the engine, but still the snowmobile was anchored to the bus.

"Come on!" shouted Jack, who couldn't see the rope and was focused on the accelerator button below his thumb and the incoming bear.

The bear now raised up on its hind legs, towering over the height of the bus. The children looked up in terror at the enormous wall of muscle, ready to come crashing down on them. It was just spitting distance now. For a third time, Knievel brought down the shovel, and finally it sheared through the rope like a guillotine.

"GO!" the kids shouted all at once, huddled tight on the snowmobile trailer and shouting, "Get back!" at the bear.

Jack jammed his thumb on the throttle and the snowmobile pulled away, belching black smoke towards the bear. The noise of the machine frightened it temporarily, and the bear flopped down onto its paws. As they got the snowmobile back through the gates, the bear began to pad towards the escaping vehicle. The children watched helplessly out of the back of the trailer as the bear ran towards them. The engine screamed at full throttle, and Jack carefully picked out a line along the tracks he had made on his outbound journey.

Victoria smashed the spoon against the saucepan over and over and all the kids screamed at the top of their lungs. Between the gates and the house, the snowmobile was able to pick up enough speed to get ahead of it by just a few seconds. But Jack had to slow to a stop at the bottom of the stone steps, and in that moment the bear caught them up.

It was so close to the children now that they could smell its breath as it growled at them. Knievel, at the back of the trailer, was almost hit when the bear launched a massive swipe with its paw. He swung the shovel at it in retaliation, and the bear backed up for a second. The children scrambled off the trailer towards the front, jumping down over the metal wall around it onto the snow, and then scurrying up the steps.

The bear reared up again and only Victoria and Knievel were still trapped on the trailer, on their backs and pushing with their feet against the metal flooring to inch away from it. It was a massive tower of muscle, with paws as big as the children's heads and claws like kitchen knives. Victoria slung the saucepan at the bear's chest, and it seemed to almost disappear into its fur as it connected with the giant. Knievel sprang onto his feet and javelined his shovel into the bear's belly, but it just bounced off as if it were a toothpick. The final two children jumped off the trailer and clambered over the snowmobile to safety.

The bear padded after the final children as they darted up the stairs and into the building. As Victoria dived through the doors, Jack and Freddy slammed them shut in the bear's face. It stood at the top of the steps and swiped at the door. From the inside it sounded like a baseball bat had swung at the oak door, and the kids had no choice but to push against it from the inside.

Again and again they heard the claws slash against the wood, and Lance watched in horror as the bolt that held the door into the stone floor began to work loose.

Finally the bear relented, and from the dining room window, Dyani saw it descend the steps and slash at the seat of the snowmobile, tearing the leather like tissue paper. The adrenaline was coursing through their veins and they shook with fear, unable to even process how close they had come to death.

Chapter 14

Close the Gate

They had excitedly come to James Bay to see bears, and they had never imagined how terrifyingly close they would come. The group watched it from the dining room window, utterly transfixed. The bear had an almost magical ability to float weightlessly across the surface of the snow on its tennis-racket paws. It sniffed around the steps and then disappeared around the back of the black barn. The kids ran up the stairs to the dorm room, which overlooked the west side of the grounds, so they could see where it went next.

The bear re-emerged into view a few minutes later and swaggered towards the front gate, leaving a trail of dirty footprints in the snow as it left.

"Are we going to die here?" said Lance, the first to break the long silence.

Dyani put her arm around him. The group were lined up along the window, looking into the endless white outside. Beyond the wall was mile after mile of snowfields and rocky tundra, like sheets of paper scattered in the wind. The gate remained open and the Great White Bear sauntered through it, almost filling the gap that had only just been wide enough for a snowmobile trailer. It disappeared among the pines to the east of the road and went out of sight.

"We're not meant to die," Jack replied, slowly and assuredly. "Not today. If it was our time to die, we would have been taken. Taken by the cold, the bear... the Walrus. So many times death has touched us and then moved right along. Something or someone is looking out for us."

Victoria shook her head. "It's pure luck, if you ask me," she said.

Knievel agreed. "That bear was so close I could almost feel its fur. Another second and we'd have been killed. And where was Mr Lagrave and his gun? He was meant to be watching us from the turret. If something's looking out for us, it ain't him, that's for damn sure."

A hand slapped onto his neck, and thick fingers squeezed.

Knievel screamed, and the children spun around to see that Lagrave had silently crept into the room and overheard them.

"How *dare* you say I wasn't looking out for you!" he thundered, hurling Knievel to the floor and unbuckling his thick leather belt. His face was red with rage, and spit flung from his mouth as he roared. His huge presence seemed to fill the room, and the children scattered like ants.

He stood above Knievel and yanked his belt through the loops on his trousers, folding it in half and bringing it crashing down on the boy's back.

"HOW DARE YOU, BOY! I AM IN CONTROL!" he screamed, smacking the belt onto the wailing boy several more times until Knievel's shirt ripped and the skin bled into the white cotton.

Lagrave stopped the onslaught and turned to the rest of the group, who had backed against the walls of the dark room. His eyes full of menace, he approached Freddy.

"You. You're the hero, aren't you?"

He jabbed his arm towards Freddy and grasped his fingers around his throat, choking him. With great power and aggression, Lagrave hurled the young man against the wall, Freddy's head cracking the white plaster around the fireplace.

"You *urinated* on the gates of Fort Lagrave! The gate that my ancestors forged from iron. HOW DARE YOU!"

Freddy shook with fear, turning his head to the side and closing his eyes as he braced for a beating.

Mr Lagrave clamped his left hand around the boy's neck and squeezed, draining the colour from his cheeks. Freddy gasped for breath as his face turned purple and his eyes bulged.

"You opened it. You need to go close it," the Walrus said, his mouth so close to the boy's face that his stubble scraped Freddy's skin. With his free hand, the monster raised his belt slowly above his head, ready to wrap it round Freddy's face.

"No!" screamed Dyani. "Please don't do it!" she begged. Victoria held her back, knowing Lagrave was ready to attack anyone and everyone who got within striking distance.

At that point, something inside Lance snapped.

"*You* close it," he said, his voice barely louder than a whisper.

The Walrus paused, wondering if he had heard correctly. He turned slowly and narrowed his bloodshot eyes, barely able to comprehend the audacity of the smallest boy in the group. He relinquished his grip on Freddy's throat, and the boy fell to the floor gasping huge lungfuls of air and clutching his neck.

"What did you say, boy? I didn't hear you," Lagrave said menacingly, stalking towards Lance and snapping the leather belt between his hands.

"I said, 'You close it,'" Lance repeated.

"I'll kill you first, boy. Should have done it days ago when I caught you outside," said Lagrave, the venom dripping from his tongue. His face was scarlet and his eyes bloodshot and wide. The young boy recognised that despite his slow movements, his fuse was well and truly lit. He was just within arm's reach when Lance continued to speak.

"Your ancestors built this place, stone by stone. Bolt by bolt."

Lance stared at the incoming murderer, who could not comprehend why a child was talking back to him. And yet Lance continued, gaining in confidence with every word.

"Your ancestors wrought those gates from solid iron, carved this magnificent estate from the very rock of heaven."

"YES! They did! And what of it, boy?" the great monster said, his head twisting sideways as the words entered his booze-soaked brain.

"*You* are the great *legend* of Fort Lagrave," continued Lance, more animated now. He stared at the psychopath as he backed up to the door that led to the landing. Lance reached behind his back and turned the brass doorknob, pushing it open. He continued to retreat onto the gallery at the top of the stairs, and

Lagrave stalked forward in lockstep like a jaguar ready to pounce.

Lance raised his arm and pointed at the painting of an old man posing with a rifle. "They are watching down on you from the walls with great pride in their hearts." His voice was now loud and confident. He spoke theatrically, not to the beast who punched and stabbed, but to the child within him who sang rhymes about bears.

The Walrus walked towards the boy through the doorway onto the landing, his eyes now wide as the words flowed into him.

Lance nodded and continued to talk, to the absolute shock of the rest of the group, who crept through the bedroom door and joined them on the landing. It was the second time today that Lance had been chased down by a beast, but this time he stood his ground and stared him in the eyes.

"People will travel from New York City to see the bravest man that ever there was. Not the bear. Not the manor. The MAN. The man who walked out of that door into the storm. The MAN who stepped fearlessly into the valley of death. And closed the gate to protect the magnificent Fort Lagrave. They are watching you."

Lance snapped his arm straight and extended his index finger towards the painting, amplifying his point.

"Today, a Lagrave LEGEND is born."

The rest of the kids were startled, their hairs raised on the backs of their necks. Lance seemed to have become possessed in the way Lagrave himself had done so many times.

The Walrus looked around the entrance hall as if he had just arrived in a time machine and was seeing it for the first time. He looked up at the painting of Pierre-Luc Lagrave in 1805, and down at his hands. He seemed surprised to see a belt in them, seemingly disconnected now from the memory of beating a schoolboy just moments ago.

The silence was broken by Lance, who stamped on the balcony. It echoed through the vast atrium, and the entire group was transfixed on him, cocking their heads in confusion. Everyone except for Mr Lagrave, who was consumed with threading his belt back through the loops on his olive-green military trousers.

Lance stamped a second time and said rhythmically, "He's going to close the gate."

Again, he stamped his foot on the floor, louder this time, and said, "He's going to close the gate."

Knievel joined him, stamping in time and singing out, "He's going to close the gate." As the Walrus did up the buckle, all six children were stamping their feet like a tribe going to war, singing, "He's going to close the gate. He's going to close the gate."

The landing shook like thunder, and for the first time since they had arrived, the Walrus actually smiled. He looked around at the group, nodding his head to the rhythm and widening his eyes. He stomped on every stair to the rhythm of the din, raising his knees and marching to the beat. As he passed another painting of a distant ancestor in the hallway, he paused to salute it, then grabbed his rifle, which was leaning against the stuffed polar bear.

He lifted his coat from the hook and turned a precise 90 degrees towards the front doors. He raised his powerful leg and kicked them open. The wind and snow blasted into the hallway, and out into the wild marched the Walrus, clomping down the steps and swinging his hulking boots over the snowmobile.

The children stopped their chant and ran down the stairs, slamming the door shut. The bolts were sheared from the wood at the top and bottom of the great oak door, and Jack and Knievel took the initiative to slump with their backs to it to keep it closed.

Freddy looked at Lance and nursed his red neck. Tears rolled down his cheeks, and the bully now looked broken.

"That," said Victoria, with one arm pointing up at the painting at the top of the stairs and the other on Lance's shoulder, "that was the bravest thing I've ever seen."

Lance smiled appreciatively, but his stomach was painful with cramps caused by anxiety. The adrenaline surged around his veins, and he had to sit on the base of the stuffed polar bear to regroup himself.

The two boys backed against the front door heard the engine of the snowmobile roaring into the distance. "Go see what he's doing, Dyani!" said Knievel, who could not leave his post without the front door blowing in.

Dyani and Victoria ran into the dining room to look out of the window, shouting updates to the doormen.

"He's driving towards the gate. No sign of the bear, but I can't see much beyond the gate. He's stopped to close the gates now, but... wait, I think it's jammed open now. Too much snow and it doesn't look like he took a shovel. He's kicking snow away to close the gates."

On hearing the word 'shovel', Victoria had an idea. She darted back into the hallway and grabbed a metal snow shovel that was leaning by the coat rack.

"Move aside," she said to Knievel, and then she placed the shovel tip-down on the hallway floorboards so that the elbow of the shovelhead was elevated, forming a shallow triangle. With both hands on the wooden handle, she slid it hard into the finger-sized gap under the door. It wedged in a few centimetres,

176

scraping angrily against the stone floor. She pulled a boot onto her right foot and stamped down on the shovel with its sole, until it was jammed in hard under the door against the granite of the steps. She got a second shovel and repeated the process on the other door.

With the entrance locked shut, Jack and Knievel stood up. It took a moment or two to realise the gravity of what she had done. Victoria looked at all the boys' faces, as if to say, 'What?'.

Knievel was inspecting his wounds in the long hallway mirror. His shirt was unbuttoned, and across the side of his ribcage were half a dozen red cuts where the leather had opened the skin.

"What if he gets mauled by the bear?" asked Jack.

"What if he doesn't?" asked Victoria, pragmatically. "It's him or us."

Chapter 15

The Battle of Fort Lagrave

"He's locked the gates. No sign of a bear," Dyani called in from the dining room window. She was back in position, monitoring the activity of Mr Lagrave, who was unknowingly trapped outside.

The others joined her at the dining room window, watching nervously as the Walrus rode triumphantly towards the house. He finally made it to the bottom of the stone steps and shut off the engine, then climbed the eight stairs and banged on the door.

"Open it!" he shouted, pounding on it furiously with the heel of his fist. The door shook as he then thumped and kicked it to get the attention of the children. The kicks quickly turned to stamps with the sole of his boots, as he began to rage and try to kick the doors down. The shovels budged slightly but were jammed hard against the ground, and with every kick the wedge grew stronger. Then he barged with his shoulder, throwing all his weight into his attack. Finally he got the butt of his gun and smacked on it with the heavy walnut stock. Still the door would not budge, and the snow shovels remained jammed in place.

"I'LL KILL YOU!" he screamed through the door. He looked towards the dining room windows, but they were too high for him to climb up to without a ladder.

He pulled out his gun and stood on the steps, just a metre from the door. He pointed it up at the top of the door, where he presumed the metal catch was holding it shut. He fired, and with a deafening blast, fragments of wood and plaster exploded into the hallway, showering the kids. There was now a hole in the door as big as a tennis ball, but still it held firm.

The children knew that they didn't have long before he made his way inside, with a gun.

"What are we going to do?" asked Freddy. "He'll get in! He'll reload that gun. There must be other entrances. Windows he can smash. Ladders he can climb up. We're done for!" he said, panicking in a way nobody had seen before.

"Let's get knives!" shouted Victoria, running to the kitchen.

"I'll go look for the tranquiliser gun," called Jack. "Lance, come with me and show me where it was kept." The two boys ran off down the east wing corridor towards the office.

The front doors shook with thunder as Lagrave smashed against them with the butt of his rifle. Dyani saw him reload the gun, and Freddy dropped to the floor with exhaustion, unable to handle another gunshot.

"Bear!" cried Dyani, who had remained at the dining room window.

"What?" said Freddy, incredulously. "The gate's locked. How?"

She had been so focused on Lagrave, just a few metres away on the front steps, that she had not noticed the bear appear over the wall near the gate. The commotion of Lagrave banging the doors had attracted it, and it had found a snowdrift tall enough to enable it to reach up to the top of the wall. The bear was so tall and strong it was able to haul itself up and over. Even at this huge distance, Dyani could easily recognise the massive outline of the Great White Bear, pouring down from the top of the stone wall into the grounds like a liquid.

It growled so noisily that the Walrus heard it over the roar of the wind. Fearing for his life, he ran down the steps and fired up the snowmobile once more. He drove it away from the stairs, cranking the handlebars full lock to the left. The bear padded towards him across the snow in front of the house.

"He's on the snowmobile!" Dyani shouted. By now Victoria had joined her, gripping a carving knife in each hand. Freddy was back to kneeling by the window, and Knievel was behind him. Lance and Jack had found the tranquiliser pistol and returned to the others, so all six of them now looked out at Lagrave thrashing his snowmobile around in a tight arc.

"Where's he going?" asked Freddy. "He's driving away from the house. Oh, wait, he's turning back. Oh jeez! He's going to ram the doors!"

Lance darted over to the massive polar bear statue in the atrium, rocking it on its wooden base towards the door. He barged his shoulder into it, but it would barely budge. "Help me!" he cried. "It must have a metal bar inside it or something. We can jam it against the doors."

Dyani and Knievel rushed to join him and pushed against it as high as they could reach, which was only around the bear's legs. Still it would not fall, despite them desperately pushing against it like rugby players.

Jack, the biggest of the group, took a run up from the bottom of the stairs and leaped up at it, using Lance's back as a springboard and launching into the beast's back. Like a bowling ball hitting the tenpin, the stuffed bear came crashing down against the front doors and wedged at an angle, with its huge paws pushing against the oak door.

Victoria yanked down the coat stand too, and with the help of Lance she dragged the heavy wooden boot rack against the door.

"He's going for it now!" shouted Freddy, who watched from the dining room window as the maniac accelerated towards the building. The engine roared at full throttle and the machine picked up speed towards the house. The skis clattered up the steps like a launch ramp and the heavy machine shot up and into the air towards the door.

Their fortifications held like a granite cliff when the snowmobile crashed into the doors. The Walrus was catapulted over the handlebars and into the wood, screaming with pain as his collarbone shattered. He clutched his shoulder as he collapsed alongside the machine, and then he tumbled back down the stone steps into the snow.

The Great White Bear padded towards him, grunting and baring its savage teeth. Lagrave rolled over in agony, pulling the rifle from his back and nestling the wooden stock into his broken shoulder. The bear reared up onto its hind legs and towered above its prey, bellowing with a bloodthirsty rage.

Lying on the ground, Lagrave closed his left eye and stared down the black barrel with his right. The front sight swung in a figure of eight as the drunk, drugged maniac desperately tried to hold his breath and stay on target. With the bear just spitting distance away, he squeezed off his round with a deafening bang.

The bullet blasted into the bear's ribs, causing it to scream in pain and fall onto its back, like an oak tree crashing to the ground. Lagrave clutched his shoulder in agony, the recoil having hammered at the broken bone. With no ammunition left in the gun, the Walrus got to his knees and scrambled through the snow alongside the building. The bear rolled back over and padded after him, swinging its huge paws and missing him by a whisker.

With adrenaline flooding his body, the Walrus reached the black barn and ran inside, slamming the door shut just as the bear reached it. He locked it shut with a top and bottom bolt, but he knew the barn would offer little protection from the massive beast.

The children ran upstairs to the dorm room where they could see the black barn from above. They watched as the Great White Bear smashed at the vertical wooden cladding of the building, tearing off planks like straw from a bale. Inside, Lagrave was using every bit of his strength to reload his gun. He took a brass cartridge from his pocket and yanked back on the bolt of the rifle to open up the chamber.

Within a matter of seconds, the bear had clawed a hole in the side of the black barn and forced its huge neck through it. It ploughed its head into the barn and thrashed it around, reaching for Lagrave with its terrifying jaws. Backed up against the wall, the man inserted the round into the rifle. The animal's teeth were just an arm's length from Mr Lagrave, but try as it might it could not get closer.

The bear retracted its head and swiped mercilessly at the barn walls, taking off so much wood that the entire side of the barn was now reduced to a pile of wood on the snow. It swung at the remaining vertical pillar, which, despite being as thick as a human leg, snapped like a matchstick. The roof crashed down onto the bear and Lagrave.

From where the children were watching, the barn looked like little more than a pile of wood ready for a bonfire. The roof and walls had collapsed, leaving a ribcage of wood in which Lagrave was totally exposed, although not completely crushed. They could see him lying on his back, pointing his gun towards the bear and waiting for the perfect shot. He knew he had one chance now to kill or be killed.

The Great White Bear tore away at the remnants of the wreckage and opened its massive, drooling mouth.

A gunshot was fired, and for a moment the kids didn't know if it had connected. The bear seemed unstoppable, and it clamped its massive jaws around the man who had been shooting it with chemicals for years. It yanked him up off the floor, dragging him through the net of wooden beams into the open air. With unthinkable violence and aggression, the bear flung his body from left to right like a salmon. The air was filled with his sickening death screams and the splitting of wood and bone.

Lagrave was torn limb from limb and his body tossed among the wreckage. The bear stood tall on what remained of the roof, its head so high that the children felt like they could reach out of the window and touch it. Its muzzle was wet with blood, and it opened its jaws and let out a deafening, hair-raising growl. The kids could see its chest had two bullet wounds, and a crimson river ran down its fur and poured into the wreckage below. In almost slow motion, it collapsed back under its own enormous weight and crashed to the ground. Its body rolled down the mountainous wreckage and slumped heavily onto the snow around it.

The children sat back on the floor, overwhelmed with emotion. Dyani was the first to cry with joy, knowing now that they could escape with their lives. Others joined her, and a wave of relief flowed through them as they realised they could return to their families after all.

Lance looked down with great sadness at the bodies of the Great White Bear and the madman who had killed him. He thought about the way chemicals had twisted them both into monsters. He felt the most sadness for Mrs Duquette, who had survived twelve years at Fort Lagrave and was killed just a day too early to experience the freedom that he felt now.

Chapter 16

The Last Tree

"Let's get out of this hole," said Victoria. "If we can get that bus started, that is. We either need to leave now or wait till tomorrow, because we have to get to that highway before nightfall.

"We can jump it from the snowmobile," she added. "They both run off twelve volts."

It was agreed by everyone that they could not face another night in this mausoleum, so Lance, Dyani and Jack coated up and went outside to search the outbuildings.

"Wait," Jack said as they went by the black barn. "We should get his gun."

Jack climbed along planks of splintered black wood and then dropped down into the wreckage. He found the body of Lagrave, torn to pieces and already frozen solid. He grimaced as he wrestled the gun from Mr

Lagrave's icy fingers, then exhaled deeply to find the inner strength to reach into the dead man's pocket to retrieve the gate key.

Meanwhile Lance crouched in the snow by the bear. It made his heart race to be so close to the massive animal. He combed his fingers through its thick, greasy fur. It was silver and shimmered like glass. With strands as long as his forearm, it was much longer than he had expected. Its eyes seemed neither dead nor alive, just black, soulless marbles that seemed unnaturally small for its head. Its bloody mouth was ringed by loose black flesh, and its canines were like yellow daggers.

Dyani stood over the body and shook her head angrily, saying aloud to nobody in particular:

"He did not agree to any of this. This bear had more spirit than ten generations of men who lived here. This man wanted money so badly that he killed for it. And now he has died for it."

She looked back at Lance and Jack, and a tear rolled down her cheek. She continued:

"There is an old Cree saying. Only when the last tree has been cut down, the last fish caught and the last stream poisoned will we realise we cannot eat money."

She closed her eyes, and the boys bowed their heads respectfully. A few moments later she climbed down from the wood stack, wiping her cheeks with her jacket sleeve.

With the rifle and gate key, the trio double-backed to the shed on the east side where the Walrus had originally instructed them to bring the bus. There they found plenty of tools and a set of red and black jump leads. Lance slung them around his neck, like heavy pythons with copper jaws. Returning to the house, they found the others had packed up their cases – including his own – and brought them to the hallway.

The group went into the kitchen and raided the larder for the journey. They could not find typical road trip snacks like crisps and chocolate, so they had to make do with tins of fruit and baked beans, along with some forks and a tin opener.

Jack and Lance made a final run to the office and rummaged through cupboards to find ammunition for the rifle. Jack took twelve cartridges and figured he would turn the weapon in to the police station when he arrived back in Matagami.

Lance looked around the office with him, flicking through piles of bills for electricity and provisions, with red OVERDUE stamped on them. The smashed-up telephone remained where the Walrus had ground it into the carpet.

They returned to the hallway and put their coats and gloves on for the final time. They hauled their bags down the steps and into the trailer, which Knievel had reconnected to the snowmobile. As was tradition, Jack drove the vehicle to the gates, and for the final time they opened them up and went out to the bus.

Victoria popped open the yellow, curved bonnet and connected up the snowmobile's battery to that of the bus. "Turn it over!" she yelled to Jack, who twisted the key in the ignition. After a few false starts, the engine choked into life and black smoke poured out of the exhaust, melting the snow around it and leaving a valley of black soot. The group cheered and excitedly climbed aboard, sitting in the same positions as they had arrived in.

"We got everything?" shouted Victoria as she let the bonnet slam shut.

"What about your sign?" Dyani asked Lance.

"Ah, that's okay. I can paint another one," he replied, not wanting to hold up the group.

"Oh really. You'll paint a polar bear out of fence paint on an eight-by-four sheet of plywood? Nah man, you gotta get that!" said Jack.

Freddy stood up and walked to the front of the bus, opening the doors and stepping off. "Hey Knievel, help me!"

To Lance's surprise, the two boys got off the bus and drove the snowmobile back towards the manor house, returning five minutes later with the sheet of wood in the trailer. With great difficulty, they wrestled it into the bus and slid it along the aisle between the rows of seats.

"Thanks, Freddy," said Lance.

"You saved my life, brother. Thank you. And sorry for your paints. And for like, everything else."

Jack reconnected the snowmobile to the tow hitch on the bus. Coordinating with Victoria, they both revved their engines, and the bus finally moved out of its rut. Once moving, they managed to get it back up to the road, where the kids had cleared a pathway. Jack dismounted the snowmobile and unhitched it from the bus, leaving the keys in its ignition.

At barely more than jogging pace – keeping the revs high so the engine didn't stall – they inched their way down the snow track that led to the James Bay Road. By the time they reached it, the time was 6 PM and they had more than four hours of driving left to go.

The return journey was quiet, as they all processed how much had changed in the five days they had been there. As they reached Wichika Springs, Victoria had collected up just enough cash off everyone to fill up the bus again.

"They'll have a phone. You think we should call home and tell them what's gone on?" Jack called back from the driver's seat. "Trouble is, they'll freak out at a fourteen-year-old driving a bus and make us wait here for the cops to come get us. Option two is we just drive right on home and deal with it there."

"Home!" they all shouted in unison.

"I'm going to phone my mom, though, and let her know we're on our way," said Lance. "I won't go into the whole story."

The others nodded. Lance fed some quarters into the payphone on the side of the building and talked briefly to his mother. He was so happy to hear her voice he was overcome with emotion, as was she.

"I can't wait to see you!" she said. "Did you bring me a painting of a polar bear?"

"Yes. Actually I did," he smiled, looking back at the massive polar bear that filled the interior of the bus.

"See you in a few hours then, honey. So Bob stayed up with you guys after all, then?"

Lance thought of the hand in the barn and was relieved when the beeps indicated that his time was up, and his call was cut off.

As predicted, when they reached home there were a lot of panicked phone calls between parents and police, as the story of murders and violence emerged.

Lance's "He's going to close the gate" speech became legendary at Delta High School. His dad beamed with pride when strangers stopped him in the supermarket to thank him for raising such a smart kid. The story of the school trip to see polar bears would be recounted for years in the town of Matagami.

Needless to say, that was the last time they sent kids up to Fort Lagrave.

Get the next book in this series of the
WORLD'S DEADLIEST SCHOOL TRIPS

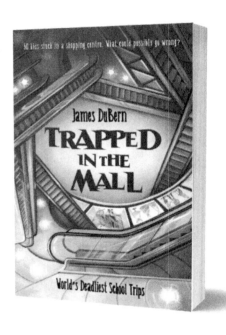

When volcanic ash smothers the UK, a coachload of teenagers take refuge in a deserted shopping centre. Food outlets are plundered, shops become homes and a makeshift city is born.

However, when resources run low, tensions rise and eventually war breaks out. Will the group be rescued before it tears itself apart?

Author's Note

I hope you enjoyed reading *The Great White Bear*. It would mean the world to me if you could review it on Amazon to help other readers discover it.

Fort Lagrave doesn't really exist, although there are real settlements built by the Hudson's Bay Company in this area (for example, Fort Albany). Traditionally, polar bears are found further north where James Bay meets Hudson Bay. However, climate change is bringing them south, to where this book is set at the southern end of James Bay.

I'd like to thank my own children Lily and Sophia, who assured me it wasn't *too* savage and have insisted that Bob the driver features in all forthcoming episodes of this book series. I'm also very grateful to Andre Cooke, who was a teenager in Matagami in the 1970s and helped me get the setting right.

If you liked this story, try Trapped in the Mall, which is twice the length and set in modern times.

Please feel free to contact me directly at james@poptacular.com. It's always great to hear from readers.

Also by James DuBern...

"Brilliantly funny story for kids and adults alike."

"The story is delightful and moves along at a great clip, keeping the reader gripped."

Rosie and her mum come up with wild ideas to get customers to visit their struggling donkey sanctuary, including creating a fake sloth and painting their horse like a zebra. Things are going well until they are exposed by Elvin McEadly, a villainous zoo owner determined to destroy their business and take their land. They now have just weeks to reinvent their business, and this time without any tricks.

Printed in Great Britain
by Amazon